Readers love the Yellowstone Wolves series by DIRK GREYSON

Challenge the Darkness

"Wonderful story, the flow and pace is perfect and kept me enthralled from beginning to end…"

—TTC Books and More

"I adored this story."

—Prism Book Alliance

"The plot as a whole kept me interested throughout the entire book and none of it felt overdone. I would very much like to see some more books come out of this 'world.'"

—Two Chicks Obsessed

Darkness Threatening

"This was another great installment in the series. I love the light and dark elements and the magical qualities that get infused into these stories."

—Open Skye Book Reviews

By Dirk Greyson

An Assassin's Holiday
Flight or Fight
Playing With Fire

DAY AND KNIGHT
Day and Knight
Sun and Shadow
Dawn and Dusk

YELLOWSTONE WOLVES
Challenge the Darkness
Darkness Threatening
Darkness Rising

Published by Dreamspinner Press
www.dreamspinnerpress.com

DARKNESS RISING

Dirk Greyson

Published by
DREAMSPINNER PRESS

5032 Capital Circle SW, Suite 2, PMB# 279, Tallahassee, FL 32305-7886 USA
www.dreamspinnerpress.com

Darkness Rising
© 2017 Dirk Greyson.

Cover Art
© 2017 Reese Dante.
http://www.reesedante.com
Cover content is for illustrative purposes only and any person depicted on the cover is a model.

ISBN: 978-1-63533-415-9
Digital ISBN: 978-1-63533-416-6
Library of Congress Control Number: 2016917546
Published February 2017
v. 1.0

Printed in the United States of America

This paper meets the requirements of
ANSI/NISO Z39.48-1992 (Permanence of Paper).

To Kate Douglas, for inspiring the entire series.

CHAPTER 1

DARKNESS WAS falling fast. Pete turned toward a rustling sound behind him before hurrying away from it. He was freaking out and he knew it.

He wanted to kill his best friend, Roger, a million times over. "Go out west, see something different—it'll inspire you." Roger's voice in his head was a full octave higher than normal, and Pete wanted to strangle it.

He just wanted to find his way back to the trail or to any sign of humanity. But that wasn't going to happen. He'd only stepped off the trail because he'd seen an amazing grove of wildflowers. How dangerous could that be? He must have gotten turned around in the damned glen and left it from a different spot than he'd come in. Now he was wandering alone at night in the middle of the wilderness. How stupid could he get?

"Don't answer that," he said to an owl calling in the trees above him.

Pete stopped under a large tree, his lungs burning, and held it for support while he caught his breath. He needed to think. But all he could think was that he was going to die and no one would ever find his body. The only people to care would be his editor and his publisher, who would wonder where his next book was. That's all. Well, and Roger, but if Pete died, he fully intended to haunt the bastard for the rest of his life. Maybe he'd crack open each can of beer in Roger's fridge so it went flat every time. Or maybe he'd poke him with a stick just when he was starting to fall asleep. Yeah, he liked that idea.

"Take that, you bastard."

He had checked his phone long ago and found no signal at all. He pulled it out again and saw a single bar. Praying to God, he dialed 911, but the bar disappeared and the call dropped. In the dying light, he looked around, and through a slight clearing in the trees, he spotted a hill and figured he should make for it. He might get a signal up there and then he could call someone. They could send a helicopter and pluck him off the edge of the precipice and just out of reach of a bear who thought he was dinner—okay, this wasn't one of his book plots. He needed to get his head in the game. In a few minutes, the light would be gone completely, so he slipped off his pack and rummaged inside it. Making the hill before nightfall was out of the question. He guessed he was stuck here for the night.

"Matches, matches…." His fingers curled around a plastic container. "Thank God." Pete looked around, found some sticks, and pulled them together in the center of a relatively clear area. That should do for him to build a fire. At least he'd have some light and a way to keep warm. He gathered tinder and some smaller sticks, opened the container of matches, struck one, and lit his kindling. The leaves caught, and Pete placed tiny sticks on top, then added a few more until he had a fire going.

"Thank you," he said, sending his vibes up toward the heavens.

Of course, the universe decided to answer and not in a good way. The sky flashed and thunder rolled over the land around him. Just what he needed.

Pete packed away the matches and continued to feed the flames, hoping the storm would go past him. As he added more sticks, the flames leaped upward enough to let him see the woodland floor around him. Lightning flashed again; the thunder grew louder and the earth vibrated with the roar of sound that died away to a growl.

It took a full second for Pete to remember thunder didn't growl. He looked up from the flames, across the clearing, and into a set of yellow eyes. That was all he could see until the cat prowled low and closer, catching the light in his thick tawny coat. A cougar. Great, just what he fucking needed. He added more sticks to the fire, then grabbed the end of a burning one, and thrust it at the cat, who seemed bold and probably hungry.

Pete's first instinct was to run, but the cat would be faster than him and pounce on his back. He had seen enough movies where the stupid kids did just that and one of them ended up as cat food.

He put a stick in the fire and added a second and a third, then pulled flaming pokers from the fire and held them in both hands. He knew it was probably stupid, but it was the only defense he had.

The cat prowled the edge of the clearing, getting closer, mouth open, displaying huge teeth. Pete jumped back and swung as the cat leaped toward him. He missed, but the cat retreated and resumed prowling and stalking him. Pete hoped there weren't more of them waiting to pounce on his back. He thought big cats like this were solitary hunters. At least he hoped to hell they were.

"Go away. Shoo." He started yelling and making noise. It was all he could think to do, waving the sticks in his hands to make himself look as big as possible. The cat hunched down, and Pete knew he was coiling his muscles for a strike. He swung both hands as the cat leaped off the ground, propelling himself toward Pete. The hot ends of the sticks connected with the cat's head, and he heard a searing sound and caught the scent of burning hair. The cat yelped and fell, then bounded off into the woods just as the sky opened up and drenched the area. The leaves of the tree overhead held off the water for a few minutes, but eventually it was too much and water poured through the thick branches.

The fire sputtered and made a valiant effort against the water, but soon it faded out, not hot enough to last. Pete took refuge close to the tree trunk, hoping for some shelter but receiving little. He was soaked through in minutes, cold, shivering, and shaken by the nearby lightning and thunder.

He wasn't sure what to do at this point. There was no shelter, and the huge tree he was under was a lightning rod in the making. Out of options and luck, he lifted his soaked pack and trudged off in the opposite direction from where the cat had gone, toward the hill he'd seen earlier. He used his phone for light, silently thanking the sales guy at Verizon for talking him into the waterproof model.

After what he guessed was ten minutes or so, the rain settled to a constant drizzle, but at least it wasn't pounding at his head and face any longer. Pete was still wet and getting colder by the second, though. He had dry clothes in a plastic bag in his pack, but they weren't going to do him much good unless he could get the hell out of the rain.

He managed to walk for half an hour in the direction of the hill, checking his phone for bars as he walked. They came and went very fleetingly, and he hoped like hell if he managed to make it to the top, he'd have a signal. Of course, that was until his phone began to chime at him that his battery was getting low. If he wanted any chance to make a call, he had to conserve what power he had left, so he slipped it back into his pocket after turning it off, plunging him into total, wet, water-sliding-down-his-back, miserable darkness.

There was nothing he could do but find whatever shelter was possible and try to wait out the rain. Pete resigned himself to spending the night out in the open. He fumbled in his pack once again, trying to remember if he had a flashlight. He should have thought about finding it before, but he wasn't doing so well in the thinking clearly department. Since he hadn't expected to be out this late or to get lost, he hadn't brought a flashlight… so that seemed to be out….

Pete closed his eyes as he checked the outer pocket of his bag and found a flat, small, giveaway flashlight he'd received from some conference or other. He pressed the button and the tiny light came on. It wasn't much, and the rain and gloom swallowed most of its glow, but it was enough to see a few steps ahead and that was all he needed. Pete figured he'd go a little farther and hoped he'd find shelter, because hope was all he had left. He slung his pack onto his back once again and wove around the trees and brush.

He was watching the ground and nearly face-planted into the corner of a structure. It was wooden, rough-hewn, and probably quite old, but Pete didn't care. As long as it wasn't a cougar den, he could deal. Slowly Pete made his way around it. His flashlight flickered, and he managed to find the door and push it open, and used the last of his light to take a look around.

It was some sort of old storage building. There wasn't much inside, but the building seemed solid and dry enough. The back was stacked with sacks from floor to ceiling, and that took up almost half of the structure's volume. The rest was empty except for some tarps lying on hay.

Pete knew hay meant that someone used this as a barn. But he hoped they wouldn't mind if he crashed here. He swept the loose hay together with his foot and spread one of the tarps over it to help soften the floor a little. Then Pete dug into his wet pack and pulled out his spare clothes. The plastic bag enclosing them was intact, so he stripped out of his soaked things and dressed quickly. He wrung out his clothes in the open doorway, then closed the door and laid them to dry over a board, knowing the owner would not thank him if he got the hay wet.

Pete pulled out his last bottle of water and a granola bar, ate it and drank half the water, then set the rest aside. How in the hell did he get into these situations? He lay down on the tarp and used another as a blanket. He was still cold, but it helped some. At least he was out of the storm, and he could listen to the rain as it beat on the roof overhead rather than onto his face. He'd had something to eat and drink. For now he was dry and safe enough, and that was all he could hope for. At first light he'd leave his shelter and make for the hill so he could get some reception and hopefully call someone to rescue his sorry butt.

Lightning flashed, illuminating the space through the single small window beside the door. Thunder rolled and wind whipped around his shelter. It sounded as though Mother Nature was letting out all her fury tonight. Pete huddled a little deeper under his tarp blanket, hoping the building remained in one piece.

Pete was weary as hell, but the storm kept him awake. Once it abated, the strange sounds from outside—including the calls and answers of wolves—scared the living hell out of him. The noises weren't near the barn, but that didn't mean very much. After the cat and now wolves, Pete would be happy to get the hell out of here and back home to New York, where he could stare at the walls for all he cared. He was never leaving the safety of the city again, writer's block or not. Writing nothing was better than losing his life and being ripped to shreds by whatever was out there.

More lightning flashed and the thunder shook the barn around him. Small bits of hay floated down from the rafters. Pete wanted to cover his head, but the tarp wasn't the best-smelling thing he'd encountered. He shook a little and prayed the storm would lessen or move on.

Unfortunately, from the sound of it, the storm seemed content to stay where it was, and more little bits floated down from above as clap after clap of thunder tried to shake his shelter apart. Pete curled into the fetal position, comforting himself as much as possible. He'd been so dumb, thinking he knew what he was doing. Even as the wind rattled the door and whistled outside, he was in much better shape than if he'd still been outside.

"Roger, if I get out of this alive, so help me, I am going to slap you silly the next time I see you. 'Go out west. Have an adventure. See things. It will spark some ideas for your next book.' Bastard!" He clenched the tarp as another peal of thunder rattled the building. They were supposed to come on this trip together. But no. Roger managed to get mono, probably from kissing every man in New York. In his raggedy, sick voice, the asshole had urged him to go on his own. *The point of this trip was so you could get ideas and stop moping around. It's a tour of Yellowstone. You'll meet people and have fun.*"

Those words rang hollow now. He had met people and gotten separated from the group. This whole thing was turning into a nightmare, and the least Roger could have done was be here to suffer along with him.

After what felt like hours, the storm moved off and it grew quieter outside. Pete rested his head on the tarp and closed his eyes. If he got a little sleep, it would help him in the morning.

Being out of the weather made Pete relax, and finally, even on the hard floor, he closed his eyes, tried to picture himself at home in his warm, soft, queen-size bed, and eventually dozed off.

CHAPTER 2

TOBIAS MONTFORD stepped out of his cabin on the small rise at the edge of a clearing and looked out over his tiny pack compound. Since reforming a few years earlier, after the devastation Anton had brought to most of the packs in the area, Tobias had done his best to provide for his pack. They'd built three habitable dwellings—well, two and a half. The last one would be done soon and the pack would be able to spread out a little. Not that it mattered terribly much.

There were only nine wolves, but his sister and brother-in-law were expecting, and he wanted them to have a place of their own to raise their pups. Lorraine was big enough to be having twins or maybe triplets, so his brother-in-law, Sasha, was working extra hard, with Tobias's help, to get the cabin finished.

The rest of his pack consisted of Clarie, his mother; Ryan Hastings, his best friend since they were pups together and Tobias's beta; Elayne, Ryan's sister; and her husband, Hayden. He also had two wolves, Greg and Brick, whose families had been members of the Greenview pack before Anton's takeover had ripped everything apart. The other former members of the pack had been scattered to the winds, while others hadn't survived the onslaught of change and the descent into chaos.

Greg strode up to him in wolf form—a beautiful, strong gray wolf—and sat on the edge of the small deck, then stared up at him and blinked. Greg preferred wolf form and was very much a wolf of night, happiest when prowling and watching the compound, keeping it safe.

"Everything okay?" Tobias asked the same question each morning and usually got the same answer.

This morning Greg lowered his head and woofed softly.

"Show me." Tobias followed Greg under the trees they'd kept for shade and to the thick woods that marked the edge of their settlement.

He sniffed and knew exactly what was bothering Greg. Someone had been through here. The scent wasn't particularly fresh, and with the storm and all the rain, they were lucky to be able to pick up the smell at all. Still, it was alarming that someone had gotten this close. He followed Greg through the compound and up to their storage barn, where Greg woofed again and walked away. Tobias stayed still, sniffing and wondering what was going on.

The intruder was human.

Greg returned a few minutes later in human form, dressed and on guard. He hated his human body. He was tall, gangly, and clumsy, knocking things over and bumbling wherever he went. But as a wolf, he was large and long, sleek and nimble. He stood ready as Tobias reached for the door, then placed a hand on Tobias's arm, and Tobias turned. "We need to tell everyone."

Shit. The last thing a human needed to see was wolves wandering the compound and shifting. They would probably faint, but then they'd know their secret.

"Go tell everyone."

Greg hurried away, and Tobias listened, hearing nothing from inside but soft breathing. Whoever was in there was asleep, or at least seemed to be. The window next to the door was fogged over, so the human had been there awhile.

When Greg returned, Tobias quietly opened the door.

A blond head was poking out from under a tarp being used as a blanket. Tobias saw and smelled wet clothes hanging over a length of wood. Over all of the smells was a woodsy scent of home that went right to his core.

"What's wrong with you?" Greg asked. "You're flushed and…." Greg turned to the sleeping man before once again looking at Tobias. "Don't even think about it." His voice was so soft, only someone with wolf hearing could pick up the words.

Whipping around to Greg, Tobias stared, his jaw set and gaze intensifying. He couldn't use his alpha voice or he'd startle the young man, but he could damn well let Greg know he was stepping over the line. Once Greg tilted his head in submission, Tobias turned back to the sleeping man and his heavenly scent.

He wanted to step inside the storage barn, lock the door to keep everyone outside, strip down, slip under that tarp, and take the smaller man into his arms. Tobias wanted him, and when Greg stepped past Tobias into the barn, he tugged Greg back behind him. Never had he laid eyes on someone and seen the rest of his life spread out in front of him. He knew he was completely and totally fucked from one end to the other. He had to be as cool and calm as possible, even though he was fairly sure Greg was aware his heart was pumping a mile a minute and he was aroused as all hell.

"Go see to the others and make sure they're okay." Though he heard Greg step away and huff, he didn't take eyes off the adorable man as he stepped inside and walked to where he was sleeping. Tobias wasn't quite sure how to wake him because he didn't want to shock the guy. He'd obviously been caught in the storm and sought shelter here.

What were the chances that Tobias would find his mate in his own storage building?

"Hello," he said softly. "It's time for you to wake up."

The man jerked upright and nearly slipped as he jumped to his feet. "I wasn't going to take anything. I was just in the storm and needed someplace dry. I'll get my stuff and be gone in a few minutes." He was already racing to grab his clothes and shove them in his still-wet pack.

Tobias held out his hands. "Slow down. I'm not going to hurt you or anything. I know the storm was bad last night. But how did you end up here?" It wasn't as though they were close to anything. The only way into their community was a two-track road that required a truck to traverse, and his pack liked it that way.

"I was taking a hiking tour and stopped to look at some flowers, and they left me. I thought I went back to the path, but I got lost and night fell. And then I tried to build a fire, got attacked by a cougar, the rain doused my fire, and I was going to try to get a cell signal, and somehow I stumbled onto your shed here, and it was dry, so.... Like

I said, I didn't take anything." He held his pack in front of him like a shield. "I can pay if I damaged anything, but I don't think so. Just point me to a road or something, and I'll walk until I can get a signal and call someone to rescue me."

The guy talked so very fast. It would have been cute if he wasn't obviously so scared. His heart beat rapidly, and the acrid scent of abject fear permeated the air.

"It's all right. Like I said, no one is going to hurt you. Come on outside, and I'll call my mom and she can find you something to eat. We don't have cell service here—it's too remote. But I can get you to a phone if you need it. I also have satellite Internet." Dang, he wanted to keep the pretty man with the bluest eyes he'd ever seen right here with him. But what was he going to do, kidnap him?

"Your mother is out here?" he said, walking toward the door with eyes as big as saucers and undertones of acrid fear in his scent.

"Yes." What did the guy think this was, a scene out of *Deliverance*? "My family is here. This is where we live." He followed the man outside and extended his hand. "I'm Tobias."

"Pete. My real name's Peter, but everyone calls me Petey. I'm not sure why that is. Everyone just has, and I went with it. But it makes me seem like a kid, and I'm not a kid, so…."

This guy clearly ran on at the mouth when he was nervous. That was adorable. "Do you want me to call you Peter?"

"Who?"

"Pete it is." Tobias's head spun as he closed the door tightly. "Come on."

He led the way to the larger of the cabins—though it wasn't much bigger than the other—which also served as the pack house and where he lived with his mom. Word had successfully gotten around that a human was in the compound, so everyone was outside, finding things to do. Tobias pulled open the door to his cabin and led the way inside to the kitchen.

"Mom."

"Honey," she said as she approached and went right to Pete. "Are you okay?" She hugged before he could react. "Come on. Let me fix you something to eat, and we can get your things dried. Then you can tell us what happened." She patted one of the stools and then began dishing out some of what she'd made for breakfast. His mother was the pack cook and loved every second of it. She was always happy when she had hungry people to feed.

"My mother likes to have someone to fuss over." Tobias pulled up the stool next to Pete, needing to get as close to him as possible. Even a few feet seemed like an impossible distance.

"Why is everyone being so nice? I mean, I'm just some guy who crawled into your barn to get out of the storm." Pete shuffled his silverware on the table.

Tobias wished he could make him more comfortable, but he was at a loss for words. Pete was his mate, and a wolf would do just about anything for his mate. He wanted to be nice to him. Hell, Tobias wanted to strip Pete down and lick him all over. If he thought he could get away with it, he'd do that right now.

Of course, his mother being in the room put a damper on that idea.

"Honey, we know we may look like people who don't have much to do with others, but we're good folk. This is harsh country out here, and the way to survive is to look after one another." She turned away and then brought over a pan of eggs.

"Are you cooking for an army?" Pete asked as she piled food on Tobias's plate. Pete requested a much smaller portion, and still she put on more than he was probably expecting. She cooked for shifters who ate a hell of a lot, all the damn time.

"No, honey. Just the group of us."

Others filed in, and she dished up the remainders and placed them on the table. Everyone lingered, mostly curious and watching Pete. Greg wasn't among them, and Tobias figured he'd disappeared into the woods to walk his patrol routes.

His mother offered Pete bacon and then took the huge platter to the table. There was toast and ham, as well as fried potatoes. Pete's mouth hung open at the amount of food, which Tobias knew wasn't going to last long. Just feeding his pack took a lot of resources, something they were barely managing to do. Pete had a little of everything on his plate, and he continued to gawk as the others divided the rest among themselves.

"Does everyone eat that much around here?" He took a bite and then ate faster. Tobias's mom knew how to cook, that was for dang sure.

"Yeah. Life out here is hard work, and it requires a lot of fuel." He tried to make light of it, even as the scent of curiosity mixed with occasional arousal as mated pairs sat together and got close. It was all normal in his house, and though he noticed it, he tried not to pay attention to it. "Once you're done eating, I'll take you to the nearest town if you want. You can call anyone you like and arrange to rejoin your group."

"How did you come to be here?" Sasha asked between bites. They were wolves, and slow eating meant someone else eyeing up the food.

"I got separated from my hiking tour. I was dumb enough to step off the path a little ways, and then they were gone. I got lost and ended up here."

"He fought off a cougar." Tobias wasn't sure why he was proud of Pete's accomplishment. "But he got caught out in the storm and stumbled onto the old storage building." He looked around at each of his wolves, then stopped at Lorraine.

She watched Pete as though he were the devil himself. She was always the one who looked for ulterior motives. Tobias caught her gaze and held it until she backed off.

Ultimately, defending his mate to Lorraine seemed pointless. To his disappointment, he was sure Pete wasn't going to be staying for very long, and Tobias had to get used to the fact that, while he'd met his mate, it wasn't to be. Tobias wasn't sure how he would deal with it, but he would. He had a pack to lead, and that trumped everything else at the moment. The pack was just starting to rebuild after the chaos and near annihilation brought about by Anton's lust for power. Anton had been put down by the current Supreme Alpha, Mikael Volokov, leader of the nearby Old Faithful pack. Mikael had supported Tobias's bid to rebuild his father's pack. That process was still ongoing, and at the moment, it took everything he had. At least that's what he told himself.

Tobias finished eating and then needed something to distract himself from his thoughts.

His mother was always so good at knowing what he needed. "Go on outside and look everything over to make sure the storm didn't do any damage." She cleared away his plate. "I'll look after your visitor, and then when you're done, you can look after him."

"I'll go with you." Sasha leaned over to kiss Lorraine and feel up her belly—and by extension, his pup—before joining Tobias. Sasha was one proud expectant papa, and it showed in the adoring way he looked at his wife each and every time.

Once they were outside, Tobias said, "It's going to be nice to have pups in the pack again." He stepped off the deck and made his way around to check the building for damage.

"I already looked, and we came through the storm just fine."

Tobias paused. "Then what's this all about?"

"The kid in there. Why didn't you just send him on his way? Everyone is nervous and jittery. Lorraine is about to launch the second Spanish Inquisition. And Clarie is acting like he's part of the family. I don't get it."

Tobias wasn't sure what kind of answer he wanted to give. Mate bonds were sacred to all wolves, especially fated ones. From that perspective, letting Pete go was a very bad thing, and normally Tobias would do everything in his power to keep him here and coax Pete into his bed just as quickly as possible. But his pack was suspicious and on edge just having Pete here, and until Tobias could explain to him and make him understand.... Hell, how did he do that and keep Pete from running screaming into the night? If he told Pete about them and he took it badly and tried to hurt them, Tobias would have to kill him in order to keep his and the other packs safe. They had hidden for hundreds of years, and they had to continue to hide what they were in order to survive. It was better for him to know Pete was out there and alive—that he had a mate—than to be the one to have to kill him.

"We're just being hospitable. Okay? If we were to be mean to him, he might tell the authorities. But right now we're just a small group of people, living on our own, and we fed him and made sure he got where he wanted to go. Just be cool and take it easy."

"If you're sure."

"What's going on?" Ryan asked as he lumbered toward them. He was a huge wolf by any standard, and if he were a natural leader, he'd have the qualities to be an alpha. But Ryan had told him long before that he liked being the right-hand wolf. He didn't want to be the one to make long-term plans and set the direction for the pack or make the big decisions. That was too much for him.

"What do you think?"

"The kid up there?" Ryan turned toward the pack house. "He's nice enough and half scared out of his wits. I don't see anything in him other than exactly what he says he is. Just some guy who got lost and stumbled on us."

"But…."

Ryan threw his arm around Sasha's shoulder. "Don't worry, bud." Ryan grinned and turned to Tobias. "I think he's about ready to go. Do you want one of us to go with you when you drop him off?"

"No. Stay here and get the cabin finished so Sasha and Lorraine can move in. Old Faithful has made furniture for it and will be bringing it over in a few days—sort of a gift to their pack neighbors—and I want it done before they come. It would look ungrateful if we have a half-finished cabin and they went to all that work to help us."

"Very good." Ryan released Sasha. "Then let's get this done. Sasha, gather everyone together and we'll get started. A day or two of hard work should get this thing done."

"Good, and then we'll start laying out one more." Tobias turned, and even though neither of them said anything, he could feel them thinking they should get started on another. Living space was precious, and they were going to need more as the pack grew. Tobias wasn't necessarily thinking that the cabin needed to be built right away, but he wanted to plan for the future. They could always enlarge the clearing, but that would leave them more exposed. "I'm thinking we'll clear some space and thin a few of the surrounding trees to make room. Let what's left provide cover for us."

"Alpha," Sasha said, turning to Tobias.

"It's long-term, not immediate. Finish the cabin, and we'll talk about the next steps." That seemed to relax him. Sasha was a great man, but making decisions and planning ahead were not his strengths. Those were Tobias's. Sasha was a good husband and would make a good, caring father, but planning would never be his forte. "I'll help when I get back."

The others streamed out of the pack house and joined Sasha and Ryan. They each knew their roles, and Ryan got them all working while Tobias hurried inside.

Pete still sat on the same stool, his eyes wide, his backpack once again clutched in front of him. "They all looked at me like I was from… I don't know… a different planet maybe."

"It's all right. We don't see many strangers out here."

"I dried your other clothes." Tobias's mother brought in the small stack and placed them in a plastic bag for him.

"Thank you." Pete stowed them in his pack and slipped off the stool.

"Come on. Let's go and get you back." Tobias's heart broke a little to say those words, but he was doing the right thing. Even though it meant saying good-bye to the one person meant for him—his fated mate—he couldn't take the chance of exposing them all.

Tobias held in the sigh that threatened to escape. If it did, his mother would wonder what was going on. And he knew if she had a clue as to who Pete was to him, she'd wring his neck for what he was doing. His mother and father had been fated mates and very happy together. When Anton defeated his father and took over, Tobias had been a teenager, and he'd done his best to hide who he was from Anton. His mother had wanted to roll over and die of grief. But they survived, and Tobias was not going to allow her to return to those times.

He led Pete to the other door and out to an old but serviceable pickup truck. It had once been blue, but now it was mostly dust- and dirt-colored. He opened the door and climbed inside, waiting for Pete to do the same. As soon as their doors were closed and Tobias was enclosed in such a small space with him, Pete's scent wrapped around him. Every time he inhaled, he scented a heady mixture of pheromones that drove him completely out of his mind.

His whole being said to tug Pete into his arms, kiss the hell out of him, and strip him naked right here on the bench seat. He turned away because his eyes threatened to shift, and damn it all if his gums didn't ache. Tobias had excellent control over his wolf and shifting. He was an alpha, after all, and he pushed back the urges and held the changes at bay. But his wolf was howling loud and clear that he wasn't going to be denied what he thought was his. *He's human*, Tobias repeated over and over, starting the engine and turning on the fan to get some outside air in to help dull his overactive libido.

"I'm sorry I disturbed you and your family." Pete still held his backpack close, and Tobias smelled fear.

"You didn't. I'm just glad you were able to get out of the storm. They can be nasty up here this time of year. Sometimes it's very dry and we get fires. Other years we get storms like that, and being outside in one is not pleasant and can be very dangerous. Lightning can take out a tree at any time, and if you're under it, that'll be the end of you."

Pete shivered, and Tobias wanted to comfort him, but he kept his attention focused ahead. It was twenty miles of rough, backcountry road, and he needed to be vigilant. The truck shook as they drove over ruts and bumps. Pete set his pack between his legs and held on.

"Have you been out west before?" Tobias asked, guessing from his accent.

"No. This was my first time. A friend and I were supposed to come together, but he got sick and urged me to come anyway." Pete was starting to turn green, so Tobias slowed down. "I'm not a very outdoorsy guy. I've always wanted to see Yellowstone and the geysers and stuff, but I didn't know that Roger had booked us on a hiking vacation until I got out here."

"He didn't tell you?"

"Nope. I think he figured I'd be too afraid to come, and he was probably right. What do I know about hiking and wilderness survival?

I got lost looking at a field of wildflowers." Pete turned away and looked out the window, breathing deeply and slowly.

"Didn't they tell you not to stray off the path?" Shit, Tobias sounded like a know-it-all prick and wished he'd kept his mouth shut. At least the ventilation was helping and his dick wasn't trying to rip through the front of his pants. But it was definitely more than interested and ached with every breath Tobias took.

"Of course they did. But I could see the path from the clearing, and everyone had stopped for a break. I took a few steps and found myself in the most amazing meadow with flowers everywhere. I figured I could just go back the way I came, but then I couldn't find it. I got turned around and I called out, but no one answered." Pete turned to him. "I don't think they liked me very much." He shifted his attention to his feet. "They were all these really big hiking people. This is what I had, and they all had these special packs. We were sleeping in cabins and things that had been booked, so we didn't need to carry tents and stuff, but you'd think they were all going for a week in the wilderness every time they left. And I was slow and kept dragging them down."

The ride smoothed out once Tobias pulled onto the main road. It was still gravel but better maintained than the track to the pack lands. Tobias sped up, and he felt Pete relax a little now that he wasn't being jostled so much. "What about the guide? He should have helped you."

Pete kept his gaze on the floor, and Tobias stopped the growl that was rising in his throat. "The first night I heard him on the phone talking to the office or something. 'Why do I always get stuck with guys like Pokey Pete?'"

"You heard him say that?"

Pete nodded, and Tobias gripped the wheel so hard, his knuckles turned white, and he felt them tingle like he was going to shift. He pushed his wolf away and the urge passed.

"Yeah. I was always bringing up the rear of the group. There were two guides with us, and that one was usually with me, but he wasn't very friendly and kept looking at everyone else like he wanted to be up with them."

"It doesn't sound like you were having a very good time."

Pete shook his head. "Some of the time I wasn't. But then we got to these waterfalls that you can only get to by foot, and they were so awesome. The water tumbled over the rocks and sparkled in the sunlight. Even the spray shone like diamonds. The others wandered around, taking pictures and stuff, while I made some notes. I'd just gotten out my camera to take pictures when the guide called to everyone that we were moving on. So I got a few pictures and then I had to go be Pokey Pete again." He finally looked up. "Is it my fault that I don't have long legs and I'm short? I tried to keep up with all those amazon people, but I had to practically run to keep up, and I couldn't do that all day. You'd think they'd set a fair pace, but nooooo…. Every day was like a forced march, and I was supposed to be having fun. Instead I was miserable. Then I see something that I really wanted to and get left behind. The bastards."

God, Pete was cute as hell when he got worked up, and Tobias wanted to shake the shit out of those guides. "Their job was to make sure no one got left behind and everyone was safe. That's what they're supposed to do. This is wild, unforgiving country, and you got very lucky last night. You fought off a cougar, and those creatures don't give up very easily. And you found shelter." Tobias smelled Pete's fear and he realized he was stoking it. "I didn't mean to scare you—I'm saying you did amazingly well." He turned quickly and smiled.

"I burned the cougar with fiery sticks. I hope he's okay. I mean, I'm glad I ran him off, but I hope I didn't hurt him too badly." He looked out the window, tensing as though the cougar could show up again at any second.

"They're pretty tough. I've had run-ins with them from time to time. You probably don't think so, but it says a lot about the way you think under pressure that you were able to fight it off."

"I don't know about that. I think I was lucky. Just like I was when I stumbled onto your barn or whatever you want to call it. I was dry and out of the weather. I waited too late to try to create my own shelter. Not that I know how to do that in the first place." He was talking rapidly again.

"No one is totally lucky out here." Tobias pulled to a stop. A fallen tree lay across the road. He got out and went to the bed, opened the box just behind the cab, and pulled out a chain saw. The tree wasn't too big, and he was able to cut it into pieces and push them off the road.

"You're really strong." Pete commented when Tobias got back in the truck some minutes later. "I don't think I know a guy who could move most of a tree like that."

"Out here you do everything you have to." He knew his answer sounded a little lame, and he chastised himself for showing Pete his wolf strength. Tobias was strong, very strong, and he probably could have lifted most of the tree off the road without cutting it.

"I see what you mean about the storm being dangerous," Pete said as they slowly moved forward past the remnants of the fallen tree. He pointed, and Tobias pulled to a stop and got out again to look. An entire field of trees had been flattened, pushed to the ground and broken off like they were twigs. It was only one small spot, but something about this didn't seem right. But he wasn't sure what it meant, if anything. He'd long ago learned to respect nature, as well as to live in harmony with her.

Tobias climbed back in the truck and put it in gear once again. "Let's go."

Something nagged at him, and Tobias wished he knew what it was. He still had a ways to go to town, so he picked up speed, and once he reached the paved road, he sped up even more. He wasn't necessarily in a hurry to get rid of Pete, but he figured it was best to let him contact who he needed to and get him back where he belonged as soon as possible. Fate was a real bitch sometimes.

Tobias pulled into the small town of Evergreen. It was more like a settlement, really. The main business was a combination restaurant, gas station, liquor store, and convenience store that stocked some basic groceries. Harold's did it all because they were all there was for a fair distance. If you wanted something unimportant, they probably didn't have it. But if there was something you needed, chances were they kept it in stock.

"Do you want some coffee or something?" It had taken quite a while to arrive.

"That would be nice."

"Then make your call and find out what they want you to do. I'm going to fill up the truck and pick up some supplies. I'll meet you inside." He got out, started the pump, and pointed toward the building. "The phone is right over there."

Pete pulled out his cell and smiled. "I have service. I'm gonna call Roger." He dialed and walked toward the entrance to the restaurant-and-bar portion of the building, then disappeared inside. Tobias finished filling the car and entered the grocery side to get what he needed.

"Hi, Harold," Tobias greeted the old man behind the counter. Harold had owned the store for as long as Tobias could remember.

"How you folks doing? Weather the storm okay?" Harold began setting things on the counter that Tobias had asked for the last time he was in the store a few weeks ago. He was a genius at getting and ordering things Tobias needed.

"Yes. Thanks. Everyone is okay and we came through just fine. You hear of anyone having trouble?"

"Not so far. But you never know. Last night was a bad one. Saw some sparks and maybe a twister, but that seems strange. We don't get those around here. Too mountainous. But stranger things have happened."

"Not lately." But odd things definitely had happened when Anton had been trying to take over. The weather, animals, and even nature herself had seemed completely out of whack. For some reason last night's storm reminded him of that time. That had to be why he was on edge. Well, that and the fact that his mate was on the other side of the wall and he was going to let him go.

"True. Things have been quiet the last few years." Harold leaned on the counter as though he were trying to be casual. "There have been a number of rumors about that. Things were really bad some years back, and then two years ago, they got dangerous, with wild, freak storms. That was about the time you and your folks started showing up around here." He straightened, and Tobias kept his expression bland and shrugged.

"There are coincidences all the time." He chuckled and walked around the store, seeing if they could use anything else. "You can't think me and my folks can control the weather." That sounded preposterous even to him, even though he was aware of some goings-on about then with the Old Faithful pack. He didn't know any of the details because the Supreme Alpha hadn't shared anything with him.

"Of course not. But folks will gab and talk about anything that strikes their fancy."

Tobias placed the rest of supplies he needed on the counter and waited while Harold rang him up. "They can talk all they want. But we aren't hurting anyone."

"I know that. You and your folks are good people as far as I can tell." Which was Harold-speak for their money was just as green as anyone's.

Tobias nodded and waited for the total. He paid in cash and then hauled the supplies to the truck. Once he'd loaded them, he ambled over to the other side of the building where Harold's wife, Florence, reigned supreme.

He loved Florence's easy manner and the way she welcomed everyone. She stood in her usual place behind the bar and greeted him when he came in. "Your friend is over there," she said rather softly and tilted her head. "You might want to rescue him from one of the local snakes."

Tobias groaned as he recognized his very own personal snake in the grass, and he strode over. "Zev." Tobias was delighted that Zev jumped up when he spoke. Sneaking up on a shifter was difficult, but Tobias had perfected the ability over the years, and with Zev, it was always unusually easy. His senses weren't the best, so he relied on brute strength and intimidation.

"Toby…." He smiled as he sat back down.

Tobias ground his teeth and looked over Zev's shoulder at Pete. He wanted to let his teeth descend and growl a warning at Zev, but it was too dangerous. Of course, Zev was well aware of that.

21

"Do you want him here?" Tobias asked Pete, ignoring Zev. Pete seemed pale, and Zev had been sitting too close for comfort. At Pete's small headshake, he said, "I think it's time for you to leave."

"Are you this one's keeper as well? You know you can't protect everyone." Zev leaned forward, way too close to Tobias's mate. That smile was pure menace, and Tobias wanted to wipe it off Zev's smug face. Instead he moved closer, caught his foot on Zev's chair, and kicked it out from under him with his far superior strength and finesse. Zev ended up flopped on the floor, and Pete placed his hand over his mouth, the curl of his smile extending around his fingers.

"Everything all right?" Florence asked gruffly from behind the bar. "I got a bat, and you better hope I don't need to use it."

"No, ma'am," Tobias said.

"I was talking to the clumsy one on the floor who doesn't seem to know how to sit down or behave. I got your bill ready. I suggest you pay and go." She wasn't someone to mess with.

Zev got to his feet. "This isn't over. You and me got a debt to settle." Zev reached in his pocket and pulled out some money. He tossed it on the bar and walked right out the door.

"Who was that guy?" Pete asked.

"The local bully." Florence strode up to the table. "I knew I never should have let that reptile in here." She handed them both a menu. "You want a drink?"

"A soda for me… and some water." Pete shifted uneasily in the chair, and Tobias saw some of the tension ease from him, but there was still a tang of fear in his scent. Tobias wished that would dissipate, but Pete seemed like the timid type.

"I'll have the same, and you can bring us each one of your famous roast beef sandwiches."

She nodded. "And I know you want double meat on yours." She turned from the table and headed back toward the kitchen.

"Do you always eat like that? If I did, I'd get as big as a house." The way Pete gawked at him was so cute. "I always have to watch what I eat because, believe it or not, I used to be very overweight and now it's a constant struggle for me."

22

"Even after all your hiking?"

"That isn't normal. I spend most of my days in my office behind my computer writing my books, or at least I used to. I haven't had a good story idea in months. That was supposed to be the reason for this trip. New experiences sometimes spark ideas for me, but it hasn't happened so far."

"What about last night? There has to be a story in that."

Pete shivered. "I'd just as soon not relive that if I can help it."

"What sorts of things do you write?"

"Well, I write general fiction, but I haven't gotten very far with it. I got a few books published, but they didn't do very well. Mostly the reviewers hated them, and the readers didn't seem to have a different opinion, so I haven't been sure what to do. So I wait tables to make ends meet."

Florence brought their drinks, and since there was no one else in the place, she stayed to talk a minute before returning to the bar when a group of local men came in. They laughed and Tobias looked them all over and discounted them as a threat before returning to Pete.

"I'll have to get one of your books. Do you write under your own name?" Tobias figured he'd order all of them as soon as he got back to his Internet connection. That way he could have a piece of his mate when he was no longer there.

"I write under Rick Gregson, but don't think you have to get them or anything," Pete answered.

Tobias committed the name to memory. "Before I forget, did you get in touch with anyone?"

"Yes. I called the tour company. They said I wandered off and didn't do what I was supposed to, and as far as they were concerned, I was on my own. They said they were happy I was okay, but that I had signed a waiver of responsibility or something." He sighed. "I'm really beginning to understand how much I hate these people."

"So what are you going to do?" Tobias's heart did a little skip, but he tamped it down.

"I don't know. They said that if I meet the group in the park on Friday at the designated time and place, they would bring my luggage and provide me a ride back to the airport. But other than that, I'm on my own for now. They were sorry I got separated from the group and offered me a free tour." He didn't sound like that was high on his wish list.

Florence brought their plates, and Pete started eating slowly while Tobias tore into his sandwich. He was dang hungry and now wished he'd ordered more food.

"Can I get fries too?" Florence nodded and went to place his order. "So what do you want to do?"

"I don't know. I could try to get a ride there." Pete set his sandwich on his plate. "I guess I didn't realize just how far we'd gone from our starting place. Florence said there's a bus coming through here that stops at the airport and she has a few rooms for rent, so I guess I'll stay in one of those and take the bus." Pete's leg bounced nervously.

Tobias didn't want Pete to leave, but this was for the best. Florence would make sure he got on the bus and see that he was okay.

That should have put his mind at ease, but it did nothing to assuage the loss he knew was coming. Wolves only got one mate, ordained by the Mother goddess herself, and when he let Pete go, he was saying good-bye to the one person in the world meant for him. He knew that and he was willing to do that for his family and pack, but that didn't mean he wasn't going to feel the loss for a very long time. "Okay. At least you'll be safe."

"You were worried?" Pete asked with a slight smile.

"Of course I was worried," Tobias said more emphatically than he probably should have. "You're a nice person who got left behind." He wanted once again to wring the necks of those tour guides. "Finish your lunch and we'll get your pack out of the truck." Tobias leaned across the table, moving just close enough that he could get a really good scent. He wanted to remember that, and the heady feeling he got, forever.

"Are you smelling me?" Pete turned to the side and sniffed. "Am I smelly or something? God, I hope not. I know I've been away from civilization for a while, but I did wash up yesterday morning before the hike. Though I didn't have a chance to clean up this morning other than to take a quick hussy bath in the bathroom while I was waiting for your mom to make breakfast." Pete twisted his hands. "Was that okay? God, I probably should have asked and all, but I didn't want to stink."

"You aren't." Man, Pete could talk fast when he got going.

"So you were smelling me?"

"I guess. You smell nice." That was the understatement of the century. Just ask his dick, which was still aching in his jeans. Damn, he quivered from sheer want. Tobias's brain was starting to cloud over as instinct and his wolf rose to the fore.

Florence brought his fries. "Will there be anything else?"

Thank the goddess that humans couldn't smell arousal, or else Tobias would want to disappear into the floor right now. "No. We're good. Thank you." He swallowed and turned his attention to his food because he needed something to do other than wonder what Pete would look and smell like when he reached the pinnacle of pleasure.

They finished their lunches and Tobias reached for his wallet, but Pete stopped him. He grabbed the check and hurried over to Florence to pay. Tobias thought it cute, but part of him balked at it. He was supposed to take care of others. It was programmed into his very being.

Pete bounded back with a smile on his face. "You've been so good to me. The least I can do is buy you lunch." He was so happy that Tobias let go of the bruise to his pride immediately. Seeing Pete smile was worth just about anything.

"Let's get your things." Tobias waited for Pete and followed him out to the truck.

Zev was close by; Tobias recognized his scent on the air as soon as he left the store, and he smelled it all the way to the truck. Tobias furrowed his eyebrows and his hackles rose as he spotted him. Pete climbed inside to get his pack, and Zev simply watched from near the corner of the store.

"He's really cute, and you'll be gone very soon and I'll be able to follow him," Zev said just below his breath as he flashed a dark smile.

25

Like most alphas, Tobias had the ability to speak directly into the minds of others. Zev must have been practicing putting up barriers, because it was harder for Tobias to reach him. However, Tobias was stronger, and just about the time a headache threatened to bloom, he broke through. *"Don't think I can't deal with you any time I want to, brother. Remember, you lost the challenge, and if you stand up to me again, I will take you out. And this time, regardless of how Mom feels, I will rip you to shreds."*

CHAPTER 3

PETE LOOKED back and forth between Tobias and Zev, wondering what in the hell was going on. Tobias was as rigid as a board and looked like he was going to eat this Zev guy for lunch. Not that Pete wanted anything to do with Zev. He was rather creepy and had these really dark eyes that made Pete wonder what kind of person he was. Not that anyone could help their eye color, but.... Jesus, he was rambling when talking to himself. *I really need to get a grip.*

"Do I need to get the ruler?" Pete asked when neither of them backed down.

Tobias stepped closer to Zev, who finally flinched a little. "No. There's no contest," Tobias said. "And Zev was just leaving." Tobias was obviously following Zev's moves with his gaze, and the intensity in Tobias's eyes and the way he kept stepping between Pete and Zev to shield him were pretty hot. Pete wondered if Tobias was protecting him. Not that Pete needed someone's protection. He could take care of himself under most circumstances that didn't involve being lost in the woods, hiking, basically the great outdoors... well, except for scaring off cougars. Apparently he was good at that. Shit, he was doing it again.

Pete watched Tobias, taking a few seconds to drink in the amazing man in front of him. Damn, Tobias was hot—really hot. Pete had always liked big guys, and Tobias fit the bill perfectly. He had muscles in all the right places. His eyes were an odd color and seemed almost yellow, but they looked amazing on him.

"If you don't mind, I think I'll take you back to the compound. Zev has a tendency to be impulsive and doesn't know when to back off."

"Are you coming to my rescue?" Pete liked that thought. He'd spent most of the morning afraid of Tobias but now realized that fear had dropped away when Tobias stood up for him.

"No. But you don't have to be back to the airport for a few days, so I can probably take you home with me, and you can spend your time doing something more interesting than waiting for the bus. That is, if you want to. You're welcome to stay here if you like."

From the way Tobias's eyes flashed, that clearly wasn't the option he wanted Pete to choose. And if he were honest, he'd been nervous at the compound, but everyone was kind enough, just reserved, except for Tobias's mother. On top of that, he wasn't really looking forward to sitting here until tomorrow and then taking an hours-long bus ride. But he definitely wasn't sure what to do.

"You don't have to do that."

"You're more than welcome." Tobias didn't step closer or pressure him, but instead flashed a brilliant, warm smile. "I'd like you to stay with us."

Pete hesitated until he looked across the small parking lot and saw that Zev guy staring at him like he was some sort of snack. The feral heat in his eyes gave Pete chills, and thinking about how it would be once Tobias left…. The chills grew. He leaned closer and lowered his voice. "How do you know him?"

"We're brothers," Zev answered from about three car lengths away.

Pete spun around, wondering how in the hell Zev had heard him. That creeped him out and made his decision for him. "Let's go." He wanted to get as far from this guy as possible.

Tobias smiled warmly and motioned to the truck. Not that he was particularly looking forward to spending another hour or more inside the truck version of a washing machine as they went over those rough roads, but he got inside and buckled himself in. "Oh God, I forgot my phone. The lady inside was charging it for me." Pete got out and hurried back inside. He walked up to Florence at the bar and smiled. "I need my phone."

"Did you want the room for tonight?" Florence asked as she handed it to him.

"Tobias said I could stay with him for a few days and then he'll take me where I need to go." He turned to the door to make sure Zev hadn't followed him inside, then swung back around.

She nodded. "He's a good man. I don't know much about him, but he's not at all like the other one."

"Thank you for everything." He gave her another smile.

"Sweetie, if I were twenty years younger…."

Pete blushed really hard. "I think you're a really nice lady, and thank you for everything." He waved on his way out, hurried back to the truck, climbed inside, and buckled up once again. He wasn't usually this scatterbrained, and he remained quiet for the first part of the trip back, not wanting to say anything really dumb.

"Is Zev really your brother?" He tried to get his head around how the two of them could be so different. Tobias was strong, but seemed caring and not selfish at all. After all, he'd driven him to town, such as it was, so he could call to get help, and now was taking him back and seemed happy about it.

"Unfortunately. He's my half brother. Zev is seven years older than me. Mom was married before she met my dad. It didn't work out between the two of them at all, and she left Zev's father a few years after Zev was born. Well, she describes it as more of making a run for her life and escaping. But then she met my dad, and they were inseparable for the rest of his life."

"But what's his problem?"

"I don't know. My dad treated him as though he were his own son. As far as I can remember, Dad never showed any favorites. But after Dad died, something changed for Zev, and he went off by himself, and that changed him too. I wish I knew what happened to him."

"He has the weirdest eyes of anyone I've ever met." The memory of those eyes still sent a chill through him. "When I sat down in the restaurant, he came right over. I knew he was coming on to me, but not in a good way." Pete looked up from his feet. "Your brother is a predator. He doesn't see people as people, but as things he wants."

He might have heard Tobias growl, but Pete wasn't sure.

"That's pretty observant of you."

"He just pulled out the chair and sat down, leaning really close. I think he thought he was being sexy, but he was just creepy." Pete shivered. "I felt like he wanted to hurt me, and I had no intention of going anywhere with him." He tilted his head to look at Tobias. "Don't think I didn't see you come charging to my rescue, and that chair thing was brilliant." He winked, laughing.

"Zev isn't a nice man. Like I said, Dad treated him the same as me, but Zev always seemed to resent that he wasn't his son."

"Did he ever meet his real father?" Pete sort of felt sorry for Zev, in a way. He knew what it was like not to know his father.

"Yes, he did. But I don't know the circumstances. Not that it matters now. His father is dead, and unfortunately Zev doesn't have much to do with Mom either." Tobias pulled to a stop. "My family is a little strange."

"No stranger than anyone else's, I'm sure." Pete turned so he could watch Tobias drive. He really liked observing him, and when Tobias turned the wheel, his shirt bunched just enough to show off the mouthwatering muscles below the fabric. Damn, Tobias was hot as all get-out. He might be the sexiest man Pete had ever met in person. He'd seen movies and stuff with really gorgeous men, but someone like Tobias had never crossed his path before.

"Are you watching me?"

Pete blushed and turned away quickly. He didn't want Tobias to be angry and didn't know for sure if Tobias was interested. Pete knew he needed to do a better job of keeping his eyes to himself. From experience, he understood straight guys didn't like gay guys looking at them. At least the ones he'd encountered hadn't. "I'm sorry."

Tobias touched the hand Pete left resting on the seat. "Nothing to be sorry for."

Pete thought he saw Tobias shiver. Now that was pretty amazing. Could a guy like Tobias be interested in him? At least Pete wasn't going to get his ass kicked. That was a relief. Hell, every few minutes Tobias kept looking over at him, so maybe if he played his cards right, Pete might just get to see exactly what was being hinted at under Tobias's shirt. "You're just being nice."

"I'm never that nice." Tobias slowed the truck at a stop sign and gave Pete the once-over, his gaze raking him from his head to his knees.

Pete squirmed when Tobias paused at his hips. Well, he guessed he didn't have to worry about looking any longer. "What do you do… for a living, I mean?"

"Mostly we live off what the land will provide. Greg is a talented woodcarver, and we have a website that I designed and built to sell his work. I do a lot of that sort of thing for other groups in the area."

Tobias was being vague, and Pete wondered why. Not that it was any of his business what Tobias did. He turned away and smiled as a thought sprang into his head: maybe Tobias built porn sites or something. Of course, he didn't ask if that was the case, but the idea stuck in his head. He'd met a guy at a party who worked as a video editor, who had confessed that he worked his way through college editing porn. He said it paid the bills and he didn't have a bunch of student loans when he graduated.

"I suppose that's real nice. I don't live off anything except my job as a waiter. I saved for months to go on this vacation."

"Do you want to be able to live off your writing?"

"Yeah, but most people can't make a living off writing alone. That takes a lot of time and luck." He held on as they drove onto the gravel road. "So I work as a waiter in a nice restaurant. The money is pretty good, but most people treat you like you're some sort of servant, and if there's something wrong…." Pete shook his head. "I had this lady two weeks before I left. She ordered the cordon bleu. I don't know why, because she said she was lactose intolerant. Cordon bleu sounds fancy, but it just means it's chicken with some ham and cheese in it." Pete snickered and then started to laugh. "I brought her what she asked for, and from the way she acted, you'd think I was stupid. Somehow she expected us to make the dish with cheese she could eat."

Tobias started laughing as well. "Let me guess—that was all your fault."

"You better believe it. The old biddy and her friends left me a dollar tip on a hundred-dollar check. I ran myself ragged for them." He continued laughing. "That was okay, though. I saw her and her friends the next week, and when I made up their bill, I added the tip on right away.

I figured if they asked, I'd tell them it was a new policy. Either that or an old battle-ax surcharge." Tobias laughed, and Pete loved the rich, warm sound. "They didn't say a word and left me a regular tip on top of it. I figured it made up for the week before."

"You little devil. It's always the small guys you have to look out for."

"I don't know about that." The truck hit a rut, and Pete bounced in his seat. Tobias didn't seem to notice. "I hope my lunch stays down," he muttered. He wasn't feeling sick, but dang, this road was enough to stir things up quite a bit.

Tobias slowed down, and the rocking became less intense. "We're about ten minutes from the… compound."

"Are you sure about this?" It was a little late to ask, but the closer they got, the more nervous he became. "Your sister didn't like having me there. She's—"

"Yes. Lorraine thinks she's the guardian of everything that's important. I love her to pieces, but she can be a royal pain in the ass when she wants to be." Tobias pulled to a stop at the only intersection for miles. "If she gives you any crap, just stare her down and don't take it. All you have to do is stand up to her and you'll be fine."

"But isn't she pregnant?"

"Yup, and I think that's made her even more protective. See, everyone there is like family, whether we're related or not. It's how we prefer to live. Being alone, we're exposed and vulnerable, but in a group, with people looking out for each other and caring for each other, we all have one another's backs, so we're that much stronger."

"I don't understand all this commune stuff. That's what you are, isn't it?" He was trying to get a picture of how things worked, and he wasn't getting very far.

"Well, sort of. But it isn't like that completely. We have a hierarchy." Tobias's speech became measured, as though he were trying to decide what to say and what not to.

"I suppose. You're the leader… right?" That, Pete was pretty sure of, with the way the others deferred to him.

"Yes. It's part of my nature to lead."

"How do you decide? Do you get elected or something?"

Tobias chuckled, and Pete wondered what that meant. "It's something like that. Zev wanted to be the leader, except all he's interested in is power over others, not actually leading and helping them build safe and secure lives. See, being a pack leader isn't about power and telling people what to do. It's about helping make sure we're all working together. Sasha is a good builder, so he helps maintain the buildings and is in charge of constructing the new cabin. He and I built the barn we found you in this morning. Brick is a very good hunter, so he brings home most of the game. Mom is the best cook you'll find anywhere, so she's in change of most meals. Of course, that means she doesn't do it all. She gets help when she needs it. Like I said, it's about working together."

"I can see that. But—" Pete wasn't sure he'd heard right. "—pack?"

"Just a group of people working and living together." Tobias made the final turn, and they were back where they'd started. He pulled into the drive next to a huge red truck that hadn't been there when they'd left. Tobias tensed as they got out and walked to the side of the main building. "I wasn't expecting you quite this quickly." He shook hands with a man even larger than he was, while Pete stayed off to the side. He didn't want to intrude.

"We had some free time and the weather was good, so we brought a housewarming gift for your sister and brother-in-law, as well as some help."

"I appreciate that. Thank you." Tobias turned in his direction, and the newcomer smiled, though it was fake or at least somewhat forced. "This is Pete. He got separated from his hiking group and was lost in the storm last night. Unfortunately the group he was with were dicks, so he's spending a few days with us, and then I'll take him to the meet-up point for his trip home."

Pete thought that was a lot of information to give as an introduction.

"Pete, this is Mikael. He and his… family, live on the other side of the valley about forty miles or so from here."

Pete extended his hand, and the huge man took it. "It's nice to meet you." The power, both physical and of his presence, was nearly overwhelming. It was like this man could do anything he damn well pleased and there wasn't a thing Pete could do to stop him. Ultimate intimidation.

"Likewise."

Pete wasn't quite sure what he should do. Thankfully Clarie came out of her cabin, so Pete got the supplies Tobias had bought and carried them inside for her. Tobias seemed busy, and Pete didn't want to interrupt anything.

"You're back?" Clarie asked with a warm smile, and Pete told her what happened. "Don't worry, honey," she said as Pete followed Tobias with his gaze through the window. Tobias walked across the compound with Mikael, the two of them deep in conversation. "Everything is going to be fine. Those two just have a lot to discuss."

"Okay." He still had a hard time looking away, and it wasn't until Tobias walked out of sight, no longer visible through the large window, that he was able to gather his attention and remember what he was supposed to be doing.

"Do you know how to cook?" Clarie asked from the kitchen.

"Oh, yes. I'm very good at that. At one time I wanted to be a chef, but I ended up a waiter instead, and now I'm trying to write books." He helped Clarie unpack the purchased supplies and let her put things where they went. "What would you like me to do?"

"I have venison for dinner and I was going to make stew, but I'm thinking it's too hot for that." She set out the huge cuts of meat, and it was on the tip of Pete's tongue to ask how big the army was that they were cooking for, but then he remembered the amount of food at breakfast.

"We can roast it. There's time, and it should come out really well as long as we season it right." Pete was happy to have something to do. Tobias had been nice enough to give him a place to stay for a few days until it was time to go home, but he didn't want to just stand around and do nothing. So he helped Clarie even as he peeked out the window every now and then to catch a glimpse of Tobias.

"I think I have things well in hand. Why don't you go out and see what's going on? You don't have to be here in the kitchen all day,"

Clarie said, wiping down the counters. They had the long-cooking items in the oven and other things were prepped and waiting.

Pete thanked her and went outside, though he stayed near the house because he didn't want to get in anyone's way.

The partially finished cabin was a hive of activity.

"Pete," Tobias yelled.

He was shirtless, and Pete swallowed hard. His corded muscles rippled as he raised his hammer, and his tanned skin, bright eyes, and a sheen of sweat made Pete's head spin. For a second, Pete tried to make his mind work. His body had ideas of its own, and he was already walking across the yard before he could think about it, like Tobias was some sort of siren.

"How is it going?" He mentally kicked himself for sounding simple. "I've been watching you all work on the cabin, and you sure seem to know what you're doing."

"We brought some experienced people," Mikael said. "And Toby here has some great folks."

"Tobias," Pete corrected without thinking about it. Both Mikael and Tobias widened their eyes. Pete had seen Tobias's reaction when Zev called him Toby, and he hated that Mikael was doing it too. "Sorry." He didn't know why he'd said anything. He usually wasn't a really forward person. "I like Tobias better than Toby. It sounds stronger."

Speaking of strong…. Tobias set down his hammer, and Pete wanted to lick him from the divot at the base of his neck, down his plated chest, and along the waistband of his low-riding jeans.

"Tobias is a good man and I think a great deal of him." Mikael looked around, and Pete realized everyone had stopped work and was staring wide-eyed at him. Pete had no idea what he'd done to get such a reaction, and he stepped a little behind Tobias, wanting to disappear. Mikael turned to the others and nodded. Slowly they went back to work, murmuring among themselves.

"Do you want me to help?" Pete asked. He wasn't particularly good with tools, but he'd try.

"That would be great," Tobias said. "Come on. I'm setting the last of these shingles, and you can give me a hand. The shakes are all cut, so if you could bring them up to me, that would be a huge help." Tobias climbed the ladder, and Pete picked up some of the shingles.

"Use one of the carriers," Mikael said, pointing to what looked like a wooden toolbox.

Pete nodded and began filling the box. Once he was done, he carefully climbed the ladder. Tobias was up near the peak of the roof, and Pete wasn't so sure about climbing onto it. The roof was steep and he wasn't that surefooted at the best of times.

Tobias came down and met him. Pete expected him to take the shingles, but he helped him up to the top of the roof where two other boxes of shingles waited on a small platform. "Did you really need my help?" There didn't look to be that much left to do.

"You're helping. You're keeping me company." Tobias placed a shingle and fastened it down with quick, practiced movements.

"It's a great view from up here." Pete could see the lay of the land now from his perch sitting on the peak of the roof. The little settlement stood on the top of a slight rise. Looking over some of the smaller trees, he said, "There's an empty field over there with flowers."

"Yes. That's where the pack used to live."

Tobias kept working, and Pete took in what was now grass and wildflowers. Tobias had explained the use of the term, but "pack" still struck him as strange.

"When do you think the house will be done?"

"This is the last of the exterior, and most everyone else is working to finish the interior, so hopefully tomorrow."

"Are Mikael and his friends staying?" Pete turned and spotted the massive man carrying boards inside. Each of them had to be heavy, and he wielded four of them as though they were nothing.

"They'll go home after dinner." Tobias reached for another shingle and paused. "Mikael is a really good man and a great leader."

"Then he shouldn't be putting you down." Pete placed his hands on his hips.

"He called me Toby. You know, my mother calls me that sometimes."

"So did Zev and he's a snake." He probably wasn't being totally reasonable, but the way Mikael had said it set Pete's teeth on edge. And damned if he could rationalize why.

Tobias smiled. "It's okay. Mikael was using it with affection. He's a good friend, and he understands what it means to be a leader. We respect each other."

"Okay." Pete turned, looking down the lines of shakes so Tobias wouldn't see him blush.

"Do you do that a lot?"

"What?"

"Blush. I think it's really cute."

"Cute?" Pete snapped much more loudly than he intended, and his voice carried out and echoed back. He continued a bit quieter. "I don't want to be cute. I'm not a stuffed animal. I am a man, you know. Just because I'm not as big as a house and don't have muscles on top of muscles and am not hot enough to light a fire and look like...." He tried to remember where he'd been going with this. He'd started talking about muscles and his mind went off in a completely different direction. "Oh, yeah... doesn't mean I'm just cute." Pete realized that others had gathered around the outside of the cabin, looking up at them and his cheeks heated terribly. He was miffed, bordering on mad, and embarrassed as hell.

"But you are cute."

Pete ground his teeth and leaned closer. "How would you feel if you weren't all this?" He waved his hand dramatically in front of Tobias. "What if you were small and slight and had bullies picking on you your entire life? I bet you never got pushed into a locker in high school and had someone shut it on you. How many times were you late for class because you had to wait for someone to let you out of a locker?"

The smile fell from Tobias's lips and his eyes heated, but Pete was too angry. "If anyone, ever... *ever*... tries to hurt you again, I swear, I'll rip them to pieces." Tobias's eyes shone and he seemed to grow even larger. Tobias tugged him close, and before Pete knew what was happening, he was being kissed within an inch of his life.

He had been kissed before and it had been nice enough, but this one was all power and heat that spread through him like a wildfire. Pete clung to Tobias, not wanting to fall, and hoped like hell this went on forever. He was so excited, his pants hurt.

Tobias held him tighter, pulled back, locked his gaze onto Pete's, and then dove in, kissed him even harder, and cupped his head to hold him still.

Pete was completely floored. The heat of the sun, added to the fire being stoked from inside, made Pete think he was going to burst into flame at any moment. He wound his arms around Tobias's neck and forgot he was on top of a roof with a man he'd known for less than a day. All that mattered was that this felt so right.

Catcalls broke through the fog that had settled around him, and Pete pulled back, blushing even more as he realized everyone was still watching them. Most seemed to be smiling, including Mikael, but Lorraine's expression was thunderous.

Pete turned away. "I should get you more shingles." He slowly made his way back to the ladder and hurried down. He wanted to disappear, but when he looked up at Tobias, he saw his huge grin. Pete ignored everyone else and brought another load of shingles to Tobias, trying not to look at him as he handed them up. This time he didn't let Tobias lure him to the top of the roof. He'd had about enough of all this extra attention. He descended the ladder and piled more shingles into the carrier.

"What do you think you're doing?" Lorraine asked as she lumbered up to him a few minutes later. Pete had hoped to stay out of her way.

"Excuse me?"

"Kissing him like that in front of everyone." She had the same yellowish eyes as Tobias—in fact, as everyone here seemed to—and hers blazed with anger. "Part of his job as leader is to find a woman, marry, and have children. It's what he's supposed to do, and with you here, turning his head, that's never going to happen." Her voice was incredibly soft, but the menace in it was crystal clear.

"So this is all about your brother being gay? Isn't that a little backward and closed-minded? Tobias can be whoever he wants to be, and I don't think that's any of your business." He drew himself to his full height—a whole five and a half feet.

"I'll decide what my business is." She stood in front of him, feet planted, hands on her hips, belly jutting out in front of her. He'd heard people say that pregnant women were eating for two. Well, this one was obstinate enough for two.

"I don't think so. I'm here as Tobias's guest, and I don't think this is how he or your mother think guests should be treated. So I suggest you back off. Tobias is a nice man and I like him."

"I don't like you being here."

"Why? Because he kissed me?" He didn't give her a chance to answer. "No, it's something else—we'd barely been introduced before you were glaring at me this morning at breakfast. So unless I somehow hurt you or farted on your best dress, I'd say you aren't being very rational." He gathered up the last of the shingles and got them together in case they were needed. Pete had to do something so he didn't say too much. He might have already.

Once he was done, he turned around. Lorraine appeared as though she'd been slapped down. Her posture was slumped and she rubbed her belly as though it ached. "Are you okay?" Pete immediately went into mother-hen mode. "You look pale."

Her face contorted, and Pete guided her over to a bench outside the nearest finished cabin. "I'll be right back." He raced to where Tobias was getting off the roof. "I think Lorraine is going into labor. We need to get her to the hospital right away."

"Sasha," Tobias called, and Sasha hurried over. Tobias relayed the information, and Sasha took off for where Lorraine was sitting and helped her inside. As if some silent call had gone out, Clarie and the other woman made their way over and disappeared into the building.

"I don't understand," Pete said, and Mikael took him aside.

"The hospital is over an hour away by car and the road is too rough. So generally children are born at home. But as I understand, if she's giving birth, then Lorraine is early." He didn't seem as concerned as Pete thought he should be. "Don't worry. She'll be fine. Lorraine is a strong wo… woman."

"SHE'S RESTING," Clarie said when she came out ten minutes later. The men had gathered outside and were waiting nervously. "Lorraine isn't in labor and just needs to rest and get off her feet. She's been doing more than she should."

"Thanks, Mom." Tobias turned to the rest of them. "Let's get back to work so we can finish this cabin and give Lorraine and Sasha a quiet place."

They all returned to work. Now the roof was complete, and only the inside was left. It wasn't a huge space, and Pete stayed outside so he wasn't under foot.

Tobias joined him. "There are too many people in there already."

"Are you finishing the inside or letting the logs show?" he asked as he helped Tobias clean any remaining materials.

"The logs mostly, although one room will have finished walls. They're doing that now and putting in the bathroom."

Pete had noticed that the dwellings were fairly simple and devoid of a lot of conveniences or fanciness. It was like they only needed or wanted simple things in their lives.

"Do you want to go for a walk? I can take you over to the clearing."

"Don't you have more work to do?" Pete didn't want to be a problem.

"Everyone is nearly done for the day." He took Pete's hand, entwining their fingers. "Dinner will be in an hour."

"I should help your mom."

"She and Elayne have everything under control." Tobias squeezed his fingers. "Mom insisted she was fine."

Pete nodded and stepped into the cover of the trees with Tobias.

"I know the way very well." There was a slight path through the trees, and it wasn't long before they broke into the wide, flower-covered clearing he'd seen from the roof. But now that he was closer, he realized the dark shapes he'd thought were dirt were actually the remains of walls and foundations.

"This is the old settlement?"

"Yes. It was destroyed a number of years ago, at the same time as my father's death." Tobias slowly walked across the clearing. "This was once the home where I grew up. All that's left is this part of the fireplace. Everything else was burned away." Tobias ran his fingers over the blackened stone.

"I'm sorry a forest fire...."

"It wasn't that kind of fire." He sighed. "Look closer. This area was burned, but all the surrounding trees are old. It only burned here, and it was very hot—enough to crack masonry and leave very little behind."

"So it was deliberate?" Pete felt... something in this space. Maybe it was his imagination, but even though the sun shone overhead, there was a sense of oppression and darkness here, like this was where sadness lived and reigned.

"Yes. Zev's father was the one who set it." Tobias slowly turned.

"Was he trying to get even with your mother for leaving?" Pete said, remembering what Tobias had told him that morning.

"In a way. Many people died here. Some of us were able to get away, but there were plenty who didn't." Tobias walked around some of the foundation stones.

"That explains why, when you rebuilt, you chose a different place."

Tobias nodded. "There were some who wanted us to rebuild here, to show that we'd overcome what happened. But I thought that this should remain as it is. Let the dead lie here undisturbed. Eventually I imagined the forest would reclaim it, but it hasn't. Not a single tree has entered the circle, and there are no sprouts either. Only flowers grow here."

"Wow." Pete closed his eyes and felt the air vibrating around him with a strange energy. "There's an underlying peace here as well as the sadness. Like those who died have found what they needed. They aren't restless but content being near their family even as they miss them." How he knew that, Pete had no idea, but he did just as surely as he knew his own name. It was both shocking and comforting at the same time. He should probably be freaking out about it, but it felt so normal for this place. "Do you come here often?"

"Sometimes. It's hard because of what I lost here." Tobias knelt next to a small pile of stones. "I still miss him."

"Of course you do." Pete came up behind him and placed his hands on Tobias's rock-hard shoulders. He was surprised at the way Tobias had opened up in front of him. He hadn't expected the huge, strong man to let out his emotions so freely. "I never knew my parents—either of them. But as a kid, I used to wonder all the time what they were like. I was told they were killed when I was a baby, but that's all I know. That doesn't mean I don't miss them." He leaned closer and put his arms around Tobias's chest. "I know it's not the same thing."

Someone coughed behind them, and Pete looked up.

One of the men stood at the edge of the clearing but didn't step inside. "Clarie said that dinner was ready and asked me to get you."

"Okay, Brick, thanks." Tobias stilled. "You know you can come in here."

Brick shook his head and looked at the other side of the clearing before turning away and disappearing into the trees.

"He lost his entire family. My mom took him in after that. It was hard, but he needed a home just as badly as the rest of us."

Tobias moved to get up, and Pete released him and stepped away. He felt as though he'd been given a glimpse of Tobias that not many people saw. What he didn't understand was why. Tobias had just let him in; he seemed to open up in a way that said they'd known each other for much longer. And on top of that, Pete felt so comfortable with him. Given how nervous he'd been the entire time, that was very surprising.

"Let's go eat." He wanted to try to comfort Tobias, but knew there wasn't much he could do. This was an old pain, something Tobias had carried with him for a very long time, just like Pete's was. He'd learned to live with it. There was nothing he could do about finding his birth parents. He'd tried and had run into dead ends.

Pete walked to the edge of the clearing, and Tobias tapped him on the shoulder.

"The compound is that way."

He blushed and followed Tobias. At least that explained how he'd gotten lost in the first place.

DINNER WAS outside and still it was a loud affair. Lorraine joined them for the meal, then returned to the cabin as soon as she was done eating. Pete was grateful she didn't send any of her withering looks his way. Mostly the conversation centered around the cabin being built. Pete detected an undertone of caution, but wasn't sure why, or even if he was reading the situation correctly.

"Your idea of roasting the venison was genius," Clarie told him as she began clearing up.

"That was delicious," Mikael pronounced, leaning back in his chair. "Denton is going to be so disappointed he missed it."

Tobias leaned close. "Denton is Mikael's mate." He then turned to Mikael. "I expected him to come with you."

Even Pete saw the shadow that passed over Mikael's face, and Tobias let the subject drop.

"We should be going." Mikael stood and the guys who'd come with him did the same. "Thank you for your hospitality."

"And for your help." Tobias shook Mikael's hand, they one-arm hugged, and then Mikael led his men out toward the front. Immediately some of the tension that had built dissipated.

"What's between them and you?" Pete asked. "I know you like Mikael, but the two of you keep circling each other a little."

"Mikael is a good leader, but it rankles because when he's here, he's the one in charge. He's really good about it, but everyone feels it, including me, and it makes them nervous. The last time someone else was in charge.... Well, you saw the clearing."

There was more to it than that. Pete was pretty sure of it, but he couldn't say why. He was missing something and he didn't know what questions to ask to figure it out. But then again, if Tobias and his people had a secret, they weren't likely to tell him, not after knowing him for less than a day. Basically Pete figured he'd stay a few days, be grateful for the hospitality, and then go home.

Now that his belly was full, his eyelids felt heavy and he yawned, even though he tried to stop it.

"Let me show you where you'll be sleeping. It's not fancy, but it will be better than the storage barn floor." Tobias led him inside and down a short hallway. He opened a door to a room just large enough for a double bed. Rustic tables sat next to it, and there was a dresser, equally rustic, with a lamp on it. His pack had been placed on the foot of the bed. "The bathroom is right over there."

"Thanks." Pete was getting really tired. He hadn't slept much the night before and it was getting dark outside. He figured folks here went to bed with the sun and rose with it.

"If you need anything, let me know." Tobias didn't leave, and Pete saw his gaze heat. He wasn't sure what Tobias wanted, but the kiss from earlier played through his mind again and again. He wanted more of those, and more, but he was leaving in a few days, and he'd never been a one-night-stand kind of guy. Still….

Pete turned away from Tobias to try to get his errant body and swimming head under control. As he bent over the bed, Tobias's hands touched the small of his back, sending heat through him. Pete straightened up slowly and leaned back as Tobias's hands roamed around to his belly, and then his strong arms enclosed his chest. The door closed with a bang, and then all was quiet except for Tobias's breath in his ear and the beating of his own heart. "Oh, yes…."

Tobias slipped his hand under Pete's shirt, then pushed it and tugged it upward. Pete raised his arms, and Tobias pulled the shirt over his head and let it drop to the floor. Not that Pete really cared. Tobias's large hands were pressed flat against his belly and chest, stoking the heat inside, which built quickly.

"God." Pete leaned back, letting Tobias support him, giving over and letting the mind-blowing sensations take him. It was only a simple touch, but it was more intimate and caring than anything he'd felt in so very long. Tobias gently moved Pete's head to the side, licked his neck and shoulder, then blew over the wet skin with his heated breath until Pete quivered and his knees threatened to give out.

Pete didn't need to worry about falling to the floor, though. In Tobias's strong arms, he felt safe, warm, and like nothing could touch him. He clutched Tobias's arms to keep steady, and stretched as much as he could to give Tobias all the access he wanted. This was heaven. When Tobias's hands slid down his belly, he inhaled, tightening his stomach, and damned if Tobias didn't slip his talented fingers beneath the waistband of his pants.

"My knees are going to give out."

"No they aren't," Tobias rumbled in a deep voice that went straight to Pete's groin. "I have you, and I'm not going to let you fall." Tobias unsnapped the fly and slid Pete's pants down his legs to pool at his feet.

His underwear was next, and Pete tried to kick off his clothes, but he only managed to get one shoe off and then didn't care anymore. Tobias slid his hands down his belly, then along the length of his cock. Pete closed his eyes, his legs shaking with uncontainable excitement. Tobias was what he'd dreamed of and hadn't realized it.

Tobias gripped him tighter, his other hand working Pete's nipples. He groaned long and loud, telling Tobias he was with him.

"That's it. Tell me what you like. I want to get to know everything that turns you on." Tobias sucked on his ear, and Pete whimpered softly. It was hard for him to know where to place his attention. Everything and everywhere Tobias touched felt so good. A lightly pinched nipple made him groan, and a swift stroke up his cock followed by a slight lap on his earlobe was nearly enough to send him over the edge.

"Tobias… I…."

"I know. I can feel how close you are." His words drilled into Pete's head, and that was intense. It was like Tobias was right there, almost inside him, so close and intimate.

Tobias turned Pete and slowly lowered him to the bed. There was no bounce or playfulness, which matched the intensity of Tobias's gaze.

Pete could get lost in those eyes, which were now a more profoundly stunning yellow-gold than they'd been before.

"Just lie right there." Tobias laved his way down Pete's belly, hands following behind.

God, that was wonderful. Pete arched his back, his hands holding the sides of his head in case the intensity became too much. But the pressure only increased as Tobias slid his lips over the head of his cock and then down the shaft, taking him in one smooth movement. Pete writhed in ecstasy as Tobias sucked hard and more intently.

"Tobias, I don't know how long...." His attempt at a warning grew out into a groan as Tobias buried his nose in his groin, taking all of him and turning Pete into a quivering mass. That continued until he could no longer control himself and the exquisite tension released in a long cry.

Pete lay still, his eyes closed, almost unable to believe what had just happened. Tobias had sucked him off. Well, yeah, that's what he'd done, but it felt like much more than that. He'd made Pete very happy, and when he cracked his eyes open, he saw Tobias's answering smile.

"I'll help you just as soon as I can move."

Tobias chuckled deeply and then kissed him.

When they broke apart, Pete wedged himself upright to watch as Tobias tugged off his shirt. The man knew how to get naked, because within seconds he was standing in front of Pete in all his masculine glory, and damned if there wasn't plenty of glory to behold. Pete wrapped his fingers around Tobias's thick cock, stroking as he guided him in for another kiss.

"I spent most of the time in the truck wondering what was under those clothes. I think I need to get a better imagination." Because his had fallen way short.

Tobias pushed Pete back on the bed using just his kisses. Pete was willing to go wherever Tobias wanted to take him. He wrapped his arms around Tobias's neck as Tobias lifted him off the bed and propelled him up to the pillows.

"I want you." Tobias shook, and Pete found it incredibly sexy that he could make Tobias that excited.

"Me too." Pete pulled him down, kissed Tobias, and let go of the last of his inhibitions and reserve.

"I'm clean and I'd never hurt you." Tobias held him tighter, and Pete splayed his legs apart, one heavier than the other because his clothes still hung from his foot. Not that he cared. Everywhere Tobias touched, he came alive. Pete hoped this would never end.

Tobias prepared him with near-scream-inducing care and thoroughness. He entered Pete slowly, stretching and filling him as he tugged on his lips. He kissed him deeply enough that as the initial pain bloomed to pleasure, nothing short of the building coming down around them was going to make this stop. Pete just didn't care about anything other than Tobias and the soul-touching pleasure he was receiving.

Their movements quickly synchronized, and they rocked back and forth. Pete would have expected Tobias to be a strong, physical lover who used his power to his advantage. Tobias's strength was definitely there, but he was caring and didn't muscle Pete, but rather he slowly drew him higher and higher until he couldn't breathe any longer.

It had only been a few minutes since he'd come the first time, but Pete felt as though he hadn't climaxed in weeks. He stroked his throbbing cock, but Tobias took over, stroking hard as Pete soaked in the warmth of his attention. As he lay shaking, staring up into Tobias's eyes, he realized he could bask in that glow for the rest of his life.

"Sweetheart…." Tobias gasped, and Pete felt him coming inside him even as his second climax barreled into him with the speed of a train.

"Damn." Pete clutched Tobias to him as he lay on top of him, his weight steadying and reassuring.

"You can say that again." Tobias smoothed the hair off Pete's forehead. "I could make love to you every day forever." Tobias kissed him hard, and Pete forgot to be worried about the words Tobias had used. He was only here for a few days, and yes, they seemed to be great together in bed, but he didn't know about love.

After a while, Tobias stood and got Pete's shoe and the last of his clothes off. Then he climbed into the bed and tugged Pete to him. Pete hadn't actually slept with anyone in a long time, yet within minutes he fell asleep, even though all the questions he had kept running through his head.

CHAPTER 4

TOBIAS WOKE up at his usual time. He was almost always the first one awake, dressed, and out to start the day. Plus he still had plenty of work to do to get Lorraine and Sasha's cabin ready.

Pete was sound asleep when Tobias carefully got out of bed. Regardless of whether Pete liked to hear it or not, he *was* cute. He lay on his belly, the covers pushed down so they barely covered his butt. He shifted and rolled onto his side as Tobias watched, and then settled quietly. Tobias could see doing this every morning—getting to watch Pete sleep for a few minutes. Of course, that was about as stupid a notion as he could think of. Yes, Pete was his mate, and last night he'd gotten a taste of him. Now he was wondering how he could possibly let him go.

Tobias turned, went to his room, dressed, and made his way through the quiet house to greet the morning. It was still dark and his wolf was more than a little itchy, so he walked to the edge of the clearing, stripped, shifted, and took off into the woods. The first thing he did was make his way around their territory, marking it. This wasn't about hunting as much as it was about stretching his legs and letting his wolf have free rein for a while. However, the rustle of a rabbit up ahead drove him forward, and he ran it down. He was about to feast when another rustling, something much larger, caught his attention. He let the rabbit scurry off, tilting his head slightly.

Footsteps, dampened and careful but still audible, caught his attention. Something was trying to sneak up on him. Tobias turned as a figure slunk nearby. He growled and shifted into a defensive position, ready for what was to come. The cougar leaped, snarling as it hurled itself in his direction. Tobias was ready, easily batting it away and raking it with his nails. The cat cried out, snarling once again, and then took off in the direction of the settlement.

Normally Tobias would let it go, but not when it headed toward home. He gave chase, paws pounding the ground, digging in as he pushed forward. This cat was not going to endanger those he cared about. Tobias tried flanking the cat to cut it off, but it was a little too fast. More than once it dodged to one side before returning to its original path.

Tobias broke into the clearing, hot on the cougar's tail, and swiped at it as it dodged around the chairs. He smelled fear on the cat as he wove around where Pete jumped to get out of the way. Tobias heard him scream and wondered why he was out there, but he kept his attention on the cat and they plunged into the woods once more. He chased it well away from the settlement, and it wasn't until the cougar dove into one of the nearby streams and was carried away by the current that he stopped. He called out to the others as he watched the cougar try to climb out on the far bank.

He listened and heard a single answering cry. His wolf wondered what was wrong, and he ran back toward the settlement. It took him a few seconds to realize there was no answer because Pete was there. He made a wide circle to come up on his clothes, but they weren't there. Tobias peered through the trees and saw Pete standing just inside the clearing, holding his clothes.

Tobias was so screwed. How was he going to explain to his very human mate about running around bareass naked in the woods? Any of the other wolves would think nothing of it. But Pete was bound to ask a million questions, not to mention wonder about a wolf chasing a cougar through the settlement. He had seen everything.

"Pete," Tobias called after shifting, leaning against a tree.

"I'm not coming. There was a wolf and that cougar is back. Are you okay?" He sounded half-terrified.

"Yes. I'm fine. I sort of need my clothes." He couldn't help smirking, especially as Pete took a few cautious steps in his direction.

Pete finally caught sight of him and rushed up. "You're naked." He stopped and looked him over before Tobias pulled Pete to him. "I don't think this is the time for stuff like this." Pete shoved his clothes at him. "The cougar that I chased off ran through the clearing with a wolf behind it. I wish I'd had my camera because no one is going to believe it. I thought they were going to eat me or something, but they ran right past and off over there." He pointed to the other side of the clearing.

"How long ago was it?"

"Maybe ten minutes." Pete pressed into him, slid his hands down Tobias's back, and then cupped his butt. "Damn, you're hard everywhere."

Adrenaline from the chase raced through Tobias, and under different circumstances, he would have stripped Pete right there and driven him crazy until his happy yells echoed through the forest.

"Why were you out here like this?"

"I was going for a swim in the creek, and I heard the commotion, so I came back to find someone stealing my clothes." That was the best explanation he could come up with off the top of his head.

"You always walk through the woods naked?" Pete stepped back, his gaze raking over him. "You sure create quite a view." He smiled.

"Is anyone else up yet?"

"I think so, given the commotion and the fact that I probably screamed like a little banshee." Pete waited while he finished dressing. "I think I understand the whole wild country thing now. But I didn't think animals like that came so close to people. Don't wolves usually stay away?"

"They do, but we're pretty remote, so sometimes their territories overlap with ours." Tobias was really starting to get tired of all this. Pete was his mate, he could feel that deep in his soul, and yet he was scared as hell of telling him that the wolf that streaked past him was in fact him and that he was trying to protect them all from a predator. "Why don't we go get some breakfast and you can tell me all about what happened." He took Pete's hand and led him out of the woods and up into the cabin, where his mother was putting food on the table.

"I need to speak with you later," she said gently, but Tobias knew there was something important behind her words. His mother was always supportive and had his back, but her eyes blazed, and Tobias wondered what had happened.

He nodded and pulled out a chair for Pete. The others at the table all seemed a little surprised, and a few nodded. Lorraine sat at the other end with Sasha next to her, and this morning she remained quiet and subdued.

The plates of food were passed to Tobias first, and he took what he wanted, then passed them to Pete, who took small amounts by comparison. Tobias was the alpha; it was his right to be served first. Ryan, his beta, sat next to him, and usually Tobias would pass him the platters, but today he was sending a message, and everyone at the table would understand that Pete was someone special to him. He wasn't sure if they understood Pete was his one-and-only mate, but maybe some of them would begin to suspect. Ryan seemed puzzled, and Tobias was certain the two of them would talk once they were alone.

"This is really wonderful, Clarie, thank you," Pete said as he ate slowly.

The others ate and talked as usual, but with an undercurrent of curiosity.

"What are we doing today?" Brick asked. "I can smell rain on the air, so we don't have all day." He stuffed his mouth with bacon and ate quickly as Tobias explained the plan of action. As soon as Brick was done eating, he nodded to Tobias and then hurried away from the table. "I'll see the rest of you out there."

"What's going on?" Tobias asked, turning to Ryan.

"I think Brick is looking to have a little more privacy." The amused look told Tobias a lot. Brick and Greg had shared quarters for a long time, but lately their friendship seemed to have shifted. Tobias narrowed his gaze and was about to ask why when Pete nudged him and smirked knowingly.

"I think Greg has a crush on Brick that isn't necessarily returned," Pete whispered. Of course, everyone around the table heard what Pete said because of their wolf hearing, but they didn't react. Packs tended to have very few secrets. "A little distance between them will probably be a good thing."

"How do you know this?" he wondered, because Pete had been here only a day.

Pete rolled his eyes. "I saw them working together, and it's the way Greg looks at Brick. I'm sure they'll work it out."

Tobias wondered if that had anything to do with Greg spending a lot of time in wolf form. He hadn't thought much of it and figured it was Greg's personal choice. Sometimes the world was easier to deal with as a wolf. Emotions were simpler and the world much less complicated. *Shit*.... Tobias pushed his plate away. All the signs of a problem between the friends had been there, and he hadn't seen it.

"Just eat. They have to work it out between them." Pete patted his hand and went back to his breakfast.

The others at the table stared open-mouthed, including his mother. Tobias glared at each of them until they lowered their gazes. Only Ryan had a self-satisfied grin, which Tobias fully intended to ask him about.

Once the meal was over, his pack members left and Ryan stayed behind. Pete asked if he could do some laundry, and Tobias's mother showed him where the machine was on the utility porch.

"What's going on between you two?" Ryan asked as soon as Pete was gone. "I'm getting the feeling he's much more than a houseguest."

"Yeah. Pete is... well, he's my mate." Tobias wasn't going to lie to Ryan. He needed to know the truth.

Ryan narrowed his eyes, then nodded. "I thought it might be something like that. But he's human, and that complicates things."

"Yes. So I'm spending what time I have with him, and then he'll go home in a few days."

"You're going to let him go?" Ryan stared at him incredulously. "Aren't you going to say something to him? He deserves to know, and you have to tell him. He's your mate, chosen by the Mother."

"I can't. What if I do and he rejects me? That could put all of us at risk, and I can't do that. We're safe here because we keep to ourselves and no one outside our community knows about us. Secrecy is part of our safety, and more than anything, I won't put the pack in jeopardy."

"So you're choosing the pack over your mate?" Ryan looked pissed. "Mates are a gift from the goddess, and I know you think you're being noble by turning your back on yours, but don't be surprised when that decision bites you in the ass. Gifts from the goddess aren't to be dismissed lightly."

Tobias was becoming angry and Ryan knew it. Tobias could tell from his smirk and crossed arms. But Ryan was a good man and someone Tobias trusted to tell him the truth even if he didn't want to hear it. "I can't take that chance."

"So you want to play the martyr for the rest of your life? How do you think everyone would react if they knew? They'd stand behind you just like you always stand behind us. Well, everyone except Lorraine, because no one knows how she's going to react to anything. Besides, think about this. Do you really think the Mother would choose a mate for you who would actually harm us?"

"I don't know." Tobias hated admitting his confusion to anyone, even Ryan. "Do you think you have the answer?" he challenged.

Ryan took a single step back, waving his hands. "Far be it from me to question what you've decided you want to do. But I think it would be wise if you gave this some more thought. You only get one mate and that's it. I've never met mine and I've been looking." The loneliness in Ryan's voice was clear. "Look, we've been friends for years and I'd hate for you to give up your mate because you think it's best for the pack."

"But it is…," Tobias argued.

"What if it isn't?" Ryan countered directly. "What if what's best for the pack is for you to trust that the Mother has a plan and that somehow your mating is part of it?" Ryan paused, turned to peer out the window facing the new cabin, and sighed. "I need to go help them finish up the cabin." He patted Tobias's shoulder. "Don't give up your chance at happiness for us." Ryan left the room as Pete came back inside.

"What do you want me to do today? I can try to help." He looked so eager it was heartwarming.

But Tobias needed to put a little distance between them. He found it nearly impossible to think when Pete was nearby. "You're welcome to do whatever you want. I have some things I need to get done, and then I'll join you."

"Okay."

"Ask Ryan what he'd like you to do." Tobias smiled as Pete practically bounced toward the door. Then he went to see what his mother wanted. He found her in her room sitting on her chair, knitting what looked like a sock, probably for him. "You wanted to talk to me."

"Close the door." Her needles clicked more quickly, a clear sign she was nervous.

Tobias complied and then sat on the edge of the bed. "What is it, Mom?"

Her fingers stopped moving and she set aside her knitting. "It's your brother." A tear ran down her cheek.

"I saw him yesterday when I was in town. What about him? I know he's back and causing trouble."

"That's just it. He called me last night and said he wants to come home and be part of his family again. Zev said he was in trouble and that he needed us." She wrung her hands.

"Mom. You know Zev is never sorry for anything and that I can't allow him to come back. Not after what he did."

"I know that." She blinked, and the sadness in her voice ripped at Tobias's heart. "This pack is good and it's healthy, growing with care and concern for each other. Zev doesn't understand any of that at all. He only knows what he wants and nothing more."

Tobias took his mother's hands. They were rough from years of work, but still felt like the embodiment of love and care. "What do you want me to do?"

"Watch out. I'm afraid Zev is going to be coming for you. He's the oldest and he feels that the leadership of the pack should be his. It doesn't matter that the pack descended from your father's family and not his. That's the way he thinks, though I tried to change his mind." She shook, becoming more and more nervous.

"What do you think he'll do?"

"I don't know. Zev was never subtle and always preferred a frontal attack." She lowered her head. "I always wondered what I did wrong with him. I know his father was terrible and I left him, but I treated Zev the same as I did you and so did your father. The only thing I can think of is that there's too much of Anton in him. I tried to…." She put her hands over her face and began to cry. "First your father, and now him."

"I know, Mom." Tobias knew she had suffered more loss than anyone should have to. "And I'm sorry he's putting you in the middle again."

"He isn't. I know what he did and what you did because of me. By all rights you should have killed Zev during that challenge, but you showed mercy, something he'd never do, and now he's trying to play on that."

"I know, Mom. He and I were brothers, and I know you did the best you could for both of us. But Zev chose his own path when he decided to turn his back on all of us and follow his father."

"I thought I taught him right from wrong. I really tried."

The tears continued down her cheeks, and Tobias wanted to make them stop. It was on the tip of his tongue to tell her that Zev wasn't worth her tears. But he was still her son and she had a right to feel what she did. "I know you did, Mom. And Zev made his own choices—ones you aren't responsible for. Zev hasn't changed at all. He made a play for Pete yesterday when we were in town."

She wiped her eyes. "Is that why you brought him back? Of course it is. You're a good alpha, and you wouldn't want anyone hurt." She took his hand once again. "I really like him."

"Me too. But…."

"There are no buts when it comes to the heart, and I know he's engaged yours." She gently stroked his cheek. "I see it in the way you look at him. Is he your mate?"

"Mom…."

56

"A mother can tell these things."

"He's human."

"Pish. If he's your mate, then that's all that matters. Your father and I had many years together—happy ones—and I'd never give them up for anything. Even knowing how things turned out, I'd still take all the hurt and loss for those years of happiness and joy."

Tobias sighed. "I just want things to be back like they were then. I know it isn't possible, but that's what I really want for this pack and Lorraine's pups. They deserve to be happy and to have a life of stability and freedom."

"I know that." She inhaled deeply and released it slowly. "You're going to need to be on the lookout for Zev because he's going to come after you one way or another."

"I figured that, Mom."

She nodded slowly and picked up her knitting once again. "While you're at it, be sure to make yourself happy. Part of what you're remembering is the fact that your father and I were exceedingly happy. That builds and spreads its own magic."

"Thanks, Mom." Tobias left her alone and went outside to join the others. He had plenty to think about.

THE DAY turned out hot, and the rain Brick had thought was coming didn't materialize, which was normal during summer. Sometimes the storms came with lightning, starting fires but not leaving a drop of water behind.

The interior of the cabin where everyone was working felt like a sauna and smelled like a locker room.

"There's just these items to go," Ryan said, showing Tobias his list.

As they talked, Brick approached and scratched off an item—the molding in the bathroom—then went back to work.

"It seems everything is well in hand," Tobias said, more than pleased.

"Why don't you take Pete and show him the creek." Ryan winked, and Tobias would have rolled his eyes if it wasn't such a great idea.

"You up for a swim?" Tobias asked as Pete passed by with an armload of scraps. The cabin was nearly clear of work debris, and with the last tasks completed, Lorraine and Sasha would be able to move in today and the pack could celebrate another milestone.

"Let me finish this up." Pete hurried off, and Tobias met him outside. "I don't have a bathing suit."

"Neither do I," Tobias said with a wink, leading Pete into the woods and down a path that wound around huge trees that had stood for decades. The sound of water rushing over rocks reached his ears.

"Wow. That's amazing." Pete approached Tobias slowly as they reached the edge of the water.

Tobias pulled off his shirt and toed off his shoes. Then he dropped his pants and waded into the fresh water.

"Is it cold?" The heat in Pete's stare was enough to warm the water by ten degrees.

"I love it. Come on." Tobias dunked down and jumped out in time to see a naked Pete put his toe in the water.

"My God. That's freezing. All my bits will shrivel up." He stepped back, and Tobias walked to where Pete stood and gently lifted him into his arms. "Okay. It's not so bad."

Tobias cupped Pete's ass as he wound his legs around Tobias's waist, and Pete's cock pressed to Tobias's belly, definitely taking interest, cold or not. "God, you feel so good in my arms." He kissed Pete as he slowly slid down into the water. The cold didn't bother him in the least. He'd been bathing in this creek for much of his life.

"It's so cold." Pete squeezed closer, and Tobias held him. "But dang, you're warm."

Tobias was so much more than warm. He ran his hands over Pete's butt and then down his crease. Pete shivered, and Tobias wasn't sure if it was from the cold, but the moan that followed answered that question loud and clear. "I love how you sound."

"You do?" Pete blushed right there.

"Does that surprise you?"

"Well… the last guy I was with…"

Tobias attempted to stifle the growl and wasn't sure he succeeded. It was stupid being jealous of some unnamed guy from before they'd met, but the thought of anyone touching his mate had him seeing red.

"...he told me I should be quieter."

"Bullshit. Making noise when you're making love is the way the gods know we're happy and that we're doing it right. So, honey, you make as much noise as you like."

"Well, look here!" Zev's scorn slunk across the water, and Tobias turned Pete away from him so Zev couldn't see him. Damn, he should have been paying greater attention to what was around him rather than only his mate. "Looks like you're slacking off or fucking around on the job. At least you picked a good piece of ass to do it with."

Tobias's temper rose and he walked to the bank, grateful that Zev was on the other side of the creek from their clothes. He gently put Pete down and provided cover while Pete tugged on some clothes. Then he turned and prowled through the water to where Zev stood at the water's edge. He'd had enough of his brother, and this time he didn't intend to show him the mercy he had before. The last time he'd stopped for his mother's sake, but that wasn't going to happen again. When he reached the bank, he climbed out. Zev wasn't as large, but Tobias could feel the power coming off him now. Granted, Tobias was stronger, and they both knew it.

"Are you challenging me? Think carefully, because this time there will be no walking away." Tobias let his teeth descend. "I don't even have to shift to take you out."

The hate drained out of Zev's eyes, but the intensity still remained. "I just wanted to talk with you."

"We have nothing to say to each other. You were banished and that's the end of it. The next time I see you will be the last time you breathe." Tobias swung his hand, shifted it midswipe, and raked his claws over Zev's chest, shredding his shirt and leaving parallel trails of blood before shifting his hand back. "Understand—you will stay away from what's mine, and that means the pack and Pete."

"What is he to you?" Zev glared across the river even as he held his hands to the wounds on his chest.

"None of your business." Tobias puffed himself up. "You stay away from all of us."

Zev turned from Pete back to Tobias. "I'll go where I want and do what I want. You may be bigger, but I have strengths you'll never understand." He pulled his hands away as the wounds on his chest closed. "Those were nothing."

"They were a message. I could shred you before you could shift and then I'd rip you to pieces, and I doubt you can heal that with whatever tricks or darkness you're tapping into." Tobias could feel it now, rolling off Zev and pushing against him. Tobias wasn't going to back down, though, and naked or not, he stood his ground, staring until Zev blinked and looked away. "Go!" He didn't point or even move. He watched as Zev turned and walked off into the woods. Then Tobias turned around and took a step back to the water.

"Look out!" Pete screamed.

Tobias twisted in time to see Zev barreling toward him in wolf form. Without thinking, he shifted, leaping toward his brother. Zev twisted out of the way and took off toward the woods. Tobias listened to him race through the underbrush until his footsteps faded into the distance.

He turned his head upward, howling his anger, frustration, as well as his slight victory in driving Zev off. Then he turned to Pete, who stood rooted in place, as white as a sheet, his hands by his sides. Tobias wasn't sure if he was even breathing until Pete opened his mouth, screamed at the top of his lungs, and raced off into the trees.

CHAPTER 5

PETE RAN, feet pounding the ground as he tried to make sense of what he'd just seen. Tobias had turned into a wolf. God, how was that possible? Pete's lungs burned and still he ran as fast as he possibly could. Stopping meant they'd get him and do God knows what to him. When he had no energy left, he dropped to the ground behind a log and held still. He was afraid to breathe loudly in case Tobias, the wolf or whatever he was, could hear him.

He lay quiet, face turned toward the log, afraid to look in case that thing was after him. What should he do? Pete listened and heard nothing, so thinking it might be safe, he lifted his head and peered over the log.

The wolf sat on the other side, watching him, tongue lolling out. It didn't come any closer. Thank God.

"Go away. I'll just go home and forget about all of this. Now, shoo, go away."

The wolf tilted its head and didn't move.

"If you can understand me, you need to go away."

It gave him a soft woof and stood. Pete was seconds from running, and he would have if he could have caught his breath. The wolf—Tobias, whatever—moved slowly closer. Pete was stunned into immobility until the wolf rubbed against his leg, and then he pulled his hands out of the way. The wolf sat down on his foot and looked up at him.

As soon as he saw those eyes, he recognized them as Tobias's. "Are you really him?" Pete slowly lowered his right hand to the wolf's head. "Tobias?" He wasn't totally sure what he'd seen and he didn't fully understand how this could be Tobias, but then the large, powerful wolf licked his hand and rubbed against him. "I need to know that's really you.

61

That I didn't… then I can understand that I saw something that shouldn't be happening."

The wolf backed away and morphed into Tobias in the time it took for Pete to blink twice. "That really is me." Tobias's voice was heavy and thick with worry.

"How is that possible?"

"It just is. My people have been here for a long time." Tobias didn't make a move to come forward. "It's part of who we are."

"But it's not possible. I mean…."

"You just saw it, so you know it's possible."

"But how?" Pete swallowed hard. "Are you, like, a werewolf and are you going to go crazy at the full moon?"

"No. I'm a shifter, not a werewolf, and I'm not going to rip you apart at the full moon. The easiest way I can describe it is that there are two parts of me, the human and the wolf." Tobias paused as though he were trying to find the words. "I've actually never had to explain this to anyone before. So I don't have the words. It's just part of who we are."

"Okay," Pete said, still nervous.

"I need to get us out of here and back to the compound. Zev is out here somewhere. He has a real interest in you, and he isn't particularly happy with me at the moment." Tobias stilled and shifted, bringing back the large gray wolf from earlier. He whined and then turned and began walking away. When Pete stayed still, he huffed and then woofed. So Pete began following, and Tobias waited for him.

This was all out of some weird movie. It couldn't be real life. Pete started to wonder if he was actually in bed asleep and if he'd wake up from the dream any second. That was the easiest explanation. Of course, the longer he followed a wolf through the woods, the more he realized this was indeed real.

They broke through the clearing into the small compound, and Ryan approached them in a rush, skidding to stop when he saw them. Ryan looked at him and then at Tobias before returning to Pete.

"I take it you're a shifter too?" Pete figured he may as well go for the shock factor. He could deal with the reality later. "Wait, don't answer. This is too overwhelming."

He hurried to the main building, and inside he was met by Clarie, who tried to stop him, but Pete brushed past her, went to the room he'd been using, and closed the door. He sat on his bed and put his head in his hands. More than anything he needed to think. There were creatures, people, who could change their shape, and Tobias was one of them. Pete should get the hell out of here and never come back. Whatever Tobias and his group were, it was no business of his. They obviously lived separately from everyone else.... Pete shook his head. This was all too much. How could he get his head around it and why was he trying to?

Maybe he was going crazy and this whole thing was one long delusion. He thought he was sane, but what if he wasn't?

He jumped at a knock on the door, got up, and cracked it open. Tobias stood outside, dressed this time.

"Can I talk to you?"

Pete wasn't so sure that was a good idea. But this was Tobias's house, and really, if he wanted to hurt him, there was little Pete could do. He slowly opened the door and then sat back on the bed. "I don't know what to think about all this. I mean, it's like fictional characters come to life."

Tobias leaned against the door frame. "Maybe. But we're real, and we're people with the same needs and wants."

"Then why keep everything a secret?"

Tobias shook his head. "Can you imagine what would happen if people found out? The government would sweep in, round us all up, and probably put us in cages somewhere or in labs so they could study and dissect us. We can change our shape, and it's part of who we are."

"So is that the reason for all the weird animal and pack references?"

"This is a pack. It's an extended family, and we live closer and more communally than others. I'm the alpha, the leader, and Ryan is my second in command, or beta. It's my job to see that everyone is safe and to take care of them all."

"So you run things."

"Some alphas do, but I try to lead. Most wolves are content to be led and to do their part. They don't want to be leaders or have responsibility. That's how the rest of them are."

"What about Lorraine?" Pete asked. "She scares me."

"Lorraine is protective as all hell. She always has been. But it's because she's seen some pretty scary things and doesn't want the rest of us to live through them."

"Like what?"

Tobias held up his hand. "Let's not go into that now. There is plenty of time for you to learn our history if you'd like to. But just let me say that our lives aren't easy."

"But she didn't know me."

"She knew plenty. First, she knew you were human, which makes you a threat to all of us, in her eyes, and she knew you were smaller than her and not as strong. That's how wolf hierarchy works. She also knew, I think, that I was attracted to you and that you were attracted to me."

Pete widened his eyes in shock. "How?"

"She could smell your attraction, just the same way I could. In addition to be being able to change shape, we have a much better sense of smell, in both forms."

"So everyone knew that I was interested in you?" Pete crossed his legs, and fuck it all if he didn't blush. "Let me guess, they also have dog hearing and…." His cheeks burned. "And you let me go on, nearly screaming last night."

"Everyone will ignore what they hear and say nothing. There are many things that I hear that go in one ear and other the other." Tobias smirked and leaned closer. "Imagine hearing your mom and dad on a regular basis."

"Oh my God." Pete groaned and covered his mouth.

"Yeah." Tobias grew quiet for a moment, for which Pete was thankful. "Just talk to me."

"I don't know where to begin."

"Did you like me before you found out I was a wolf?" Tobias leaned closer, his voice softening greatly, and Pete's dick stood up and took notice. What was worse, he now knew Tobias could scent it.

"You know I did." He felt surly at the moment.

"I'm the same person I was then." Tobias sighed. "Nothing has changed, except now you know who I really am."

"It sounds like you're coming out of the closet."

"Maybe. There are some who have this aversion to gay people like us, but not in this pack or Mikael's, and since he's the leader of all of us, that sort of attitude has died away."

Pete nodded. "I think I need some time to think this out. It's a lot to wrap my head around, and it doesn't help that you're standing there, being all sexy."

"Okay." Tobias sighed, turned, and left the room, closing the door after him.

Pete lay back on the bed and stared up at the rustic ceiling, following woodgrain patterns with his gaze. This whole thing was so overwhelming, and yet it wasn't. What did it matter if Tobias could turn into a wolf? It wasn't like he was vicious in his wolf form. Or at least he hadn't been to Pete.

Pete closed his eyes and tried to think. He knew he was crazy for not running screaming back to the city and home. But for some reason, this place felt right to him. Lord knows Tobias was incredible, and he felt like home, which Pete couldn't figure out either. Maybe Tobias could put ideas in his head and make him think things that weren't true. Like a glamour. No, that was vampires. And if Tobias could do that, he'd have made him think he'd been seeing things and none of this was real.

The issue was, what the hell was he going to do now?

"Fire!"

Pete jumped up, left the room, and raced down through to the living area and then outside. Everyone ran into the clearing as smoke rose from the trees to the west of the settlement. "What do we do?" Pete asked Ryan after he nearly ran into him in his haste.

"Tobias went to take a look to see how bad it is and if it's moving in our direction. If it is, we'll have to get everyone into the trucks and out of here as fast as we can. Get your things together, one bag, and be ready."

"What can I do to help?" His backpack already had his things in it, so there was nothing for him to pack.

"Lorraine and Sasha," Ryan said, and Pete was already moving.

He hurried to their new cabin and pounded on the door. When Sasha opened it, Pete raced inside. "I thought I'd help."

"You!" Lorraine said from where she stood by the bed. "This is your fault, you know."

"Please." Pete glared at Tobias's sister. "How do you figure that?" He placed his hands on his hips, tapping his foot. "And do you want help or not?"

"Yes, we do. Thank you." Sasha had two old suitcases on the bed. He threw a few more things into them, then snapped them shut. "Please take those to the pack house. We'll be right behind you."

Pete grabbed the bags and left.

"That's enough, Lorraine," Sasha said as Pete hurried to the house with the suitcases, then set them with the others.

The air was still, almost ghostly so, and Pete knew that had to help. Maybe the fire would burn itself out and that would be the end of it. He turned to the cluster of small buildings and then remembered the other clearing and how sad and lonely it was.

"Ryan, do you have pumps for water?"

"Yes."

"Then get people wetting down the cabins. Hose them down, get everything as wet as possible. Other than the buildings, there isn't much to burn here."

"You've never seen one of these fires. If it comes here, it will be hotter than Hades. The cabins will burst into flames just because of the heat."

"Do you want to give up or do you want to do something?" Pete countered. That seemed to snap Ryan into action.

66

"Greg, Brick, grab the hoses and pump from the storage shed. We'll run the extra lines to the creek."

They took off, and Pete helped Clarie and the others while everyone waited for Tobias to return. After finishing and with nothing else to do, Pete paced, watching the edges of the clearing for Tobias. He had a bad feeling, and it grew worse and worse as time passed.

The hoses were laid and the men began pumping water everywhere, drenching the cabins and the pack house, as well as the ground.

"Wet it good and then get the surrounding trees. Drench everything you can reach!" Pete spoke loudly to make sure he was heard over all the other noise. The pumps must have been powerful, because they were using small firehoses, and soon water sluiced off the roofs to puddle in low places on the ground.

Pete couldn't wait anymore. "I'm going to try to find him," he told Ryan and then took off. He heard Ryan telling him to stay there, but Pete ignored him. He'd been to the creek before, and he followed the path and the hoses. It wasn't very far, after all.

What he hadn't counted on was the smoke. It was thick and hung in the trees overhead, like a ghostly gray fog blocking out the sun and creating a gloom. As he got nearer to the creek, the smoke descended closer to the ground. He reached the water's edge but could see very little beyond it. "Tobias!" Pete paced back and forth near the water. He couldn't see the flames, but he could hear the crackling and roaring, which was getting louder. "Tobias!"

Pete wondered what he should do until the ground under his feet gave way and he rolled down the bank to splash into the creek. *Well, hell.* He came up, soaked to the skin, waded across, and climbed out. Water dripped off him, but he had to find Tobias.

Your mate is this way.

The words were planted in his head, like they'd been his own thoughts, but he knew they weren't. Pete paused and then trudged through the trees toward the flames. Then he heard it—a cry and the shuffle of leaves. He had no idea why, but he knew it was Tobias.

Pete's feet pounded the ground and he burst into a small glade. Tobias was near the edge, with a snare around his hind feet and a rope that fed up into the tree above looped around his neck. Jesus, Tobias was strangling to death. Flames approached him, burning the grass, licking closer across the tiny clearing. Pete wished he had a knife, but he raced over, and stamped out the flames as best he could before forcing himself to get the rope off Tobias's neck. It wasn't working, and each movement hurt Tobias even more.

Pete followed the rope and hugged the tree. He managed to reach a low branch and hoisted himself up, and climbed as quickly as he dared. His eyes burned and he coughed from the smoke as the fire got closer, but he had one thought and that was to rescue Tobias. He reached where the rope was fastened and managed to loosen the knot, shaking with coughing fits as he worked. The rope fell away and Tobias slumped to the ground. Pete blinked, trying to see, as he began climbing down.

The branch holding his right foot snapped, and Pete hung in the tree, scrambling to find purchase for his feet. He caught his left foot on the stump of a branch, steadied himself, and then slowly climbed to the ground.

Pete got the rope off Tobias's neck and then got his back feet free from the snare. "We have to get out of here." The grass fire was getting closer, the roar of flames growing louder by the second.

Tobias was breathing, his wolf chest rising and falling, but he lay on his side and didn't get up.

"You have to move." Pete lifted his head to look into Tobias's eyes, but they were closed. He was alive, Pete knew that, but he wasn't responding otherwise. The fire crept closer, and Pete knew he had one chance. Carefully, he lifted and mostly dragged Tobias into his arms. He was heavy, and Pete stumbled and nearly fell with his first step before he balanced and headed back the way he'd come.

His eyes watered from the smoke and his lungs burned with it, but the farther away he got, the more the air near him was clear. "I'm doing the best I can, but any time you want to wake up would be good." Pete lifted his head upward. "I know I wasn't raised to believe in any particular god, but if there is one, I could sure use some help." He reached the creek and set Tobias on the bank as a low rumble from falling trees shook the forest, and he had to tamp down his rising panic. The smoke had cleared quite a bit and he needed to breathe.

"I need some help. If any of you can hear me, I'm at the creek." God, he hoped that Tobias hadn't been kidding and that everyone had great hearing. His lungs ached something terrible, and taking a deep breath made him cough. He regulated his breathing, in and out, hopefully to get rid of the smoke that was still in them.

The sky darkened and the rumbling increased. It was hard to see past the smoke overhead, but he hoped that was thunder. He thought it might have been trees exploding from the heat of the fire, and if that were true, there was little he could do for any of them. The rumble sounded again, and this time lightning flashed and the sky opened in a deluge of epic proportions. The rain came down with such force, it hurt his face. He turned and leaned over Tobias, protecting him from any pain.

A wolf appeared on the other side of the stream.

"Tobias is hurt." Pete had no idea who it was or even if it was one of Tobias's pack members.

The wolf jumped into the stream, swam across, and prowled toward him, eyes intense. Pete knew this wasn't help, but a menace on top of another.

"Get the hell away!" Pete screeched at the top of his voice.

Lightning flashed and struck the ground near the creek. The wolf yipped and jumped out of the way, his coat singed. He ran off, down the creek, and Pete returned his attention to Tobias, grateful to whoever seemed to be on their side.

"Tobias?"

"We're over here!" Pete called and saw Greg as he forded the stream.

Greg hurried up to him. "What happened?"

"Tobias was tied up and being strangled." The rain continued, but it wasn't pelting him now. "I was able to get him free, but he isn't waking up. There was another wolf. It got scorched by the lightning and ran off that way." He pointed downstream.

Greg stilled, sniffing. "Zev, that bastard."

"You can smell him?"

"Yes. The rain has nearly washed it away, but his scent is on Tobias as well." Greg lifted Tobias into his arms and slowly made his way across the stream. Pete followed, and soon they were on the other side and working their way toward the settlement.

When they broke from the trees, they were surrounded by the rest of the pack.

"You found him?" Ryan said to Greg, who shook his head.

"Pete did. He got him free and up to the stream."

"Get him in the house," Clarie instructed. "We need to get him warm and out of this weather."

No one argued as she took charge. Greg carried Tobias into the house, and Pete followed. Clarie fussed, and they lay Tobias on the blanket-covered sofa.

"What's wrong with him?" Pete sat on the sofa near Tobias's head, gently stroking it.

"I'm not sure." Clarie brought a blanket over and laid it over Tobias. "He could be worn out, and some rest will allow him to shift into his human form and heal."

"Zev was there. I smelled him," Greg offered.

"You think he did this?" Clarie asked him.

"Someone set a very definite trap, one that seemed to be designed for him because I think Tobias would know what to look for, or else they were counting on haste." Pete was babbling a little. "But I really don't know. By the time I got to him, he was choking pretty badly. I got him loose and he's still breathing, but… is there some poison that he could have used?"

Clarie inspected Tobias's neck, which appeared as though it had been burned. "The rope was spiked with silver, I'm willing to bet. He's been poisoned by it."

"What do we do?" Pete asked.

"There's nothing we can do. You removed it, and his system needs to get rid of whatever he absorbed."

"Bring me a brush, and if you are all affected by the silver, then get out. I need to brush him to make sure there isn't any more on him. That rope was in terrible shape and bits of it could still be in his fur."

Clarie got the brush, Pete began stroking it over Tobias.

"I'm going to go wash," Greg said, and they all backed out of the room.

Pete slowly worked through the hair on Tobias's head and neck, and small glittery flecks came off into the brush. He used the blanket as a catchall and continued until he saw no more flecks. Once he was done with the one side, he brushed the other and then moved Tobias off the blanket and gathered it into a wad that he took outside and left in a heap. He was going to have to dispose of it later.

"Okay, honey, I got rid of the silver, so you need to open your eyes and look at me." He checked Tobias's neck, and the wounds seemed to be healing.

"Is it clear?" Clarie asked, coming back into the room.

"Yes. I put the blanket outside the door on that side, and I'll take care of it for you later." He waited for her to come over beside him. "I think he's healing."

"Yes."

"Do you always regenerate tissue that fast?"

Clarie shook her head. "It's because he's the alpha. What happened to him would most likely have killed any of the rest of us. Now that he's healing, we need to give him some time. What he needs to do is shift. The rearrangement of his body will heal him, but he has to be strong enough to do it, and right now he can barely move."

"Can you get me some water for him?"

She hurried away, returned, and sat next to where Pete cradled Tobias's head on his lap. "I know you've been through a lot today. Is there anything you want to ask me?" She handed Pete the glass, and he set it aside for when Tobias woke and could shift back, which he hoped would be soon.

"The questions are almost too numerous to try to figure out." Pete scratched his forehead. "I guess the strangest thing is that I went out looking for him, and as I crossed the creek, I think I heard a voice in my head. It told me where Tobias was—wait, where my *mate* was…. I think those were the words used, and they weren't from me because I'd never talk like that. It would have creeped me out if I wasn't so worried about Tobias." He checked again and saw Tobias's eyes were open.

"I think those are questions you have to ask him." Clarie patted Tobias on the side. "You need to shift back," she told him, but Tobias blinked and pressed his head to Pete's chest. "Okay, now you're just soaking up the attention. I'll get you some clothes." She left, and Pete released Tobias's head and stood.

"If you're faking, I'll swat your ass good and hard!" Pete put his hands on his hips and glared at him.

A gasp sounded behind him, and he turned and stared at Lorraine's angry expression.

"You can't talk to him like that." She jabbed her finger in his direction.

"Yes, he can," Tobias said raspily, lying on the sofa, and then slowly got up.

"You wouldn't take that kind of behavior from me, but you will from the human?" She and Tobias glared at each other, and Pete took a step back out of way. It would have been almost funny the way they both growled at each other, but Pete had had enough.

"Should I get a ruler?" he quipped to try to defuse the situation.

"You will stop acting like you're the alpha of this pack." Tobias drew himself up to his full height. "And he can talk to me any way he wants. He was the one who went to find me, got me out of those ropes by climbing a tree through clouds of smoke, and then carried me to safety. He risked his life for me."

"Drop it, Lorraine," Ryan said from behind her. "He was also the one who helped Sasha and suggested we hose everything down. I'd say this man was thinking of all of us and put his safety on the line, so you might want to keep an open mind about him." Ryan took her by the arm. "I suggest you go back to your cabin, which Pete helped build along with the rest of the pack. Get back into bed and quit causing trouble."

"I—"

"Tobias is the alpha, and unless you want to challenge him, the way your idiot brother did, then back off."

She wrenched her arm away from Ryan and walked to where Sasha stood with his arms crossed over his chest. It looked like Lorraine wasn't getting any support from anyone. "Come on."

Sasha waited and let Lorraine go first, but he didn't gentle her in any way. Pete was very glad he didn't have that enhanced hearing, because the argument that was sure to happen between those two was not going to be pretty.

As Ryan left, Clarie came in, saying, "Here are some clothes." She handed them to Tobias. "I'm going to make a simple dinner so everyone can eat and get some rest." She left, heading toward the kitchen.

Tobias pulled on the sweatpants and T-shirt.

Pete glared. "Don't think about going out there. You were hurt and you need to rest. Everyone will be in for dinner. I'm sure they can bring you up to speed on everything you want to know."

"Pete—"

"Don't take that tone. Not after what happened. You scared the living crap out of me." He smacked Tobias's shoulder and then rubbed his hand. "Are you made of rocks? You sure as hell felt like it when I was carrying you."

"I did? Wait, you really care for me?"

"Yes. Of course I do. What, do you think I'm some sort of slut who spends the night with every good-looking guy who rescues me from his psychotic brother?" Pete rolled his eyes dramatically. "Of course I care about you."

"That's good." Tobias sighed, sat back down, and tugged Pete next to him.

"I'm going to miss you when I have to leave in two days." He really was. Pete took Tobias's hand, and leaned against him. This was a strong man with a huge heart. He definitely was going to miss Tobias, but he needed to get back to his real life, and maybe once he did, the weirdness that seemed to surround this place and everyone in it would recede to the background. It wasn't likely he'd ever be able to look at anyone ever again and not wonder if they were shifters like Tobias.

"I'm glad you'll miss me, because you'll take part of me with you when you go." Tobias kissed the back of his hand, and Pete wondered what that meant. So much had happened that processing it all was nearly impossible, and he had no idea what was meaningful or not.

CHAPTER 6

TOBIAS WAS exhausted, but he could feel his well of energy replenishing. He ate his dinner quickly, answering everyone's questions and reassuring them that he was all right.

"So it was Zev?" Brick asked.

"Yes. I also believe he set the fire with the hope that he could burn us out."

"Why?" Greg asked as he took care of his dishes.

"I don't know." Tobias had to be honest. Zev was a mystery to him on so many levels.

"He's jealous," Pete offered from next to him. "He's the older brother, right?"

"Yes. But it was my father who was the alpha of this pack."

"But Zev's father was an alpha as well, right? At least that's what I think I've been able to figure out. So maybe it doesn't have anything to do with this pack. Maybe he just wants to be an alpha like his father and any pack will do. And he's fixated on this one because he wants to get even with you because you defeated him in a challenge. God, trying to follow what all of you have said is getting really hard, but I hope I got it."

Tobias put his arm around Pete and tugged his mate closer. He was really wondering how he was going to survive once Pete was gone. Part of him would be hollow, and he knew that. Yes, it might be simpler if he told Pete that he was his mate, and knowing what he knew about Pete, he'd stay because Tobias needed him to. But that wasn't what he wanted. Yes, he wanted a mate, his mate, but he wanted Pete to stay because he cared about Tobias and loved him, not because he felt trapped into it. Tobias wouldn't do that to anyone, especially not his mate.

"Why don't you all tell me what happened here?" Tobias needed to get onto a different train of thought. They talked over each other to explain, but it all centered on Pete and then Ryan leading everyone to get the cabins wetted down.

Pete spoke up. "I think you should build two secure pump houses down at the river and run pipe up to the settlement. If this happened once, it will again, so bring the water right here for the future. Let's say that next time it isn't Zev but a natural fire. We still want to be able to protect the settlement. It isn't that far."

"True. Let's keep it in mind."

"Are you humoring me?" Pete asked with a lopsided grin.

"They're so cute," Elayne whispered to Hayden. Pete didn't appear to hear it, but Tobias did. He was relieved that the pack seemed to be accepting Pete on his own merit.

"I'm going to go to bed." Tobias was barely staying awake. The events of the afternoon were too much, and he needed a chance to recharge. "Please wake me if anything happens or if Zev shows his face."

"I don't think he will. The lightning strike got him pretty good. Though the smell of singed hair was rather gross."

"Ha!" With that, Tobias left the table and went right to his room. It was the biggest in the house, with the largest bed. He undressed and lay down, the aches and exhaustion catching up with him fast.

Tobias had no idea how long he was alone, but it was dark when he lifted his head as the bedroom door opened.

"I brought you some water." Pete came in and almost immediately began to swear. He managed to put the glass on the table beside the bed before hopping on one foot. "Do you have good night vision?"

"Yes."

"Well, not all of us do." Pete flopped onto the bed, holding his foot. "That really hurts."

"Let me see it." Tobias didn't turn on the light, but he cradled Pete's foot. There was no blood, so he rubbed it gently, feeling the muscles release. "The dark doesn't bother us at all, so we don't turn on extra lights at night."

"I see that. This room is pitch-black. I can barely see the outlines of anything at all." Pete groaned as Tobias stroked up his calf and then under his shorts to his thigh. "I thought you were tired."

"I've been sleeping for a while."

"I get that you're wide awake now." Pete shivered and groaned as Tobias let his hand roam farther, skimming the inside of Pete's thigh, loving the rich sounds he made. Pete reached for him. "You're naked."

"Yeah. Is that a problem?" Tobias cupped Pete under his shorts.

"Obviously not." He stroked slowly, and Pete's moans grew louder and then abruptly cut off. "What's wrong?"

"I don't want anyone to hear me," Pete whispered. "It's embarrassing."

"No. It's exciting." Tobias slipped his hands away and tugged at the front of Pete's pants. "Just think about them hearing how hot you are and how good I make you feel." Tobias growled low and long. "But they will never see or touch you. That's something only I get to do. And they will never say anything at all."

"Why not?"

"Because everyone else can hear them too. It's sort of an equalizer, and it's part of our private lives. Just because we can hear it, doesn't mean we would ever say anything. It's very impolite." Tobias tugged open Pete's pants, but Pete took his hands to stop him.

"What if Zev is out there listening?" Pete shook and Tobias tugged him close. "I hate that man. He's so creepy, and… what did I ever do to him?"

"He sees slights where there are none and the bad side of everything." Tobias rolled them until Pete was underneath him. "I will always do my best to protect you."

"How can you?"

Pete's question made Tobias pause. He'd felt like a fool for letting Zev get the best of him, and now Pete was questioning him. Tobias rolled off and lay on his back. The energy that had been building inside him leaked away like water through a sieve.

"I mean, I'm only going to be here for a few more days, and once I leave, I'll take care of myself, just like I always have."

Pete was right. There was little Tobias could do. Yes, he could tell Pete that he was his mate. Hell, he could get him over the top with passion, take him, mate with him, and then he'd feel the same draw that Tobias did. But that would be stripping away Pete's right to choose. He could also just explain things, but he'd be damned if he was going to guilt Pete into anything. No. He had to just let things happen and hope his heart and soul didn't shatter into so many pieces that he could no longer put them together again. "What's your life like back home?"

"In New York? I work five, sometimes six nights a week. It's a great city with so much to do, but it's very big. There's theater and all kinds of entertainment."

Tobias closed his eyes as Pete spoke. "How can you get to know a city that big?" Tobias had always lived in areas like this. After their family escaped from Anton's takeover of the pack, they'd lived in Cheyenne for a while. It wasn't as big as New York City by any means, but it had been overwhelming for him and Lorraine. Zev seemed to make the most of it, but Tobias had never understood why anyone would want to live that way.

"You learn your piece of it and then branch out over time." Pete shrugged. "I learned to be very self-sufficient at an early age. My parents were gone and I ended up in foster homes, so I never really had a family per se. Roger and I met in one of the homes. We became friends and have stayed that way. I guess he's the closest thing to a family I have."

"So you don't have a pack of any kind."

"No. Not all of us are lucky enough to have a pack we can count on. I learned to rely on myself and be wary of others." Pete sighed. "When I'm not at the restaurant, I'm usually trying to work on my latest novel. That hasn't been going so well lately."

"I'm sorry."

"I just don't have any ideas right now. I keep telling myself that something will come and that inspiration will strike, but it hasn't. Maybe when I get home and can sit where it's quiet and think…."

78

"Why do you write?" The creative mindset was something Tobias didn't really understand.

"I guess because I like to think I have something to say. But then maybe I'm blocked because I really don't have anything to say and I'm only kidding myself."

"I doubt that." Tobias rolled onto his side, toward Pete. "Just from what you said, it sounds like you have something to tell others. Life is hard, and not everything happens the way you expect or want it to. I lost my father—he was taken away from me—"

"How? I assume it's a wolf thing."

"Yes. Anton, Zev's biological father, wanted it all, and he attacked my father just like he challenged many of the other pack leaders in the area. They fought, and my dad lost. I still think Anton cheated somehow, and Mikael says he was using a dark magic to enhance his powers." Tobias paused.

"I know how it feels to lose your parents."

"Yes. But I watched the challenge. I was there when Anton eviscerated my father. I remember hiding my eyes and my mother nearly becoming sick. Can you see women you know going through that?"

Pete gasped. "No one should see that."

"Well, Mikael has two boys in his pack, and their mother went through the exact same thing as mine when Anton challenged and killed their father with the boys watching. It was part of the way he did things. Anton was all about bringing as much pain as possible. Thankfully those boys were young, and when I spoke to Mikael about it once, he said they have good lives now and don't really remember it."

"Jesus." Pete grew quiet. "Things seem so quiet here and idyllic... well, except for Zev."

"There's always the dark with the light. That's what Mikael told me when he asked that I rebuild this pack. After he defeated Anton, he wanted to try to rebuild all the packs. So we started a few years ago. We're still small, but we're getting there and we'll continue to grow." Tobias yawned, growing tired once again.

"It sounds like all of you have been through so much."

"We have. Greg and Brick were lone wolves until they found us, and I suspect there are more single wolves or small groups out there who need homes."

"Have you—shifters—always lived here?" Pete asked, snuggling closer, and Tobias put his arm around him.

"Yes. For a long time, we hid in caves and among humans. But we always had to be careful. Wolves had been hunted nearly to extinction, so if we shifted and were seen or caught, then we'd be advertising our presence. When the wolves were reintroduced to Yellowstone, it gave us a way to emerge again. But those years were very long and hard. Many of my forebears lived in abject poverty. We were reduced to hunter-gatherers and some subsistence farming. Many of our pups died because they couldn't get the nutrition they needed. I was born just before we came out of hiding, so I don't really remember it. But Mom and Dad told me the stories."

"Did they live here then?"

"No. There are dry caves in the hills, and they built shelters in them. We could go up there, but it isn't pretty, and the winters here are very cold and long. It was a harder life than we can imagine. So I know that, to you, what we have here is primitive, but to us, it's all we need."

"My God. When you told me, I never even thought about things like that. I know what it's like to be different and the hatred that can go along with it. People aren't accepting of gays sometimes."

"Some packs aren't, but Mikael won't tolerate homophobia in any of his, and he's very clear about it. Since he's the Supreme Alpha and stronger than any of us, it's the way it is."

"So might makes right."

"In a way, yes. Mikael also puts a heavy emphasis on leadership, but I could be challenged, and if I lost, I could be removed and someone else would lead the pack. I think I'd have the backing of everyone here and it isn't likely to happen, no matter how much Zev might wish it would."

Pete gently stroked his chest, and Tobias closed his eyes. Talking about their history always made him grateful for what they had and left him scared that they could be back there once again.

"We should go to sleep."

"Yes." Tobias hugged Pete closer.

"I'm glad you're okay." Pete kept rubbing him gently, which was both nice and incredibly intimate. His wolf wanted to do more than that, but Tobias was too tired and his mind was going in too many directions to make love. Instead he was being cared for, and he needed it.

It wasn't too often that he allowed himself to be comforted. He was usually the comforter and dealt with his own issues alone. It was part of being the alpha—strength, leadership, no weakness.

"I know you think you have to be strong, but I'm not going to tell anyone."

Tobias wasn't sure what to say, so he kept quiet. He needed to get his thoughts together and figure out what he was going to do once Pete was gone.

"I know."

And his mate, Pete, would be exactly the person he needed in a partner. He'd know when to stand up to him, when to back him up, and when he needed someone to listen. His mother had told him that was what she's always done for his father and that it had come naturally because they were mates. She'd also told him that he would be able to trust his mate with his life. Well, he was going to have to figure out how he was going to do without that. He just didn't know if he could.

He was seconds away from just telling Pete that he was his mate and that it meant they were destined to be together, ordained by the Mother herself. "Pete, I need to tell you something…."

Tobias listened, but all he got in response was a soft snore.

SOMETHING WAS wrong. Tobias wasn't sure what it was, but something didn't feel right. He listened and heard nothing, then sniffed the air and scented nothing out of the ordinary. Carefully Tobias got out of the bed so he wouldn't wake Pete. He pulled on a pair of sweatpants, left the room, and padded outside. Everything was quiet and there didn't seem to be anything out of the ordinary, except a light in the direction of the creek. Tobias stripped, shifted, and raced off to investigate.

The light grew brighter as he approached. Tobias slowed at the edge of the trees, then cautiously approached the water.

"I'm right here, Tobias." A woman in light, looking a lot like his mother, walked toward him, a carpet of green springing up under her feet as she stepped.

He huffed and tilted his head, questioning.

"Look at me. I'm the Mother of all of you."

He lowered his eyes so not to look at the goddess, then shifted forms and stood still. "Yes, I know." He raised his eyes, and the light around her dimmed.

"I have always done my best for all my children." She came closer and touched his chin. "My gifts are given because I want the best for all of you. They aren't to be ignored. He is your mate for a reason."

"Can I ask…?"

"No. If I wanted you to know, I would tell you. But Pete is your mate. He's everything you think you need, and some things you don't even know yet. To let him go would be a mistake. But I will not compel you to change your mind. In fact, I applaud your wish not to force him to stay."

"Then what do I do?"

"I'm not Dear Abby." She shook her head. "You need to look deep into your heart and figure out what you want and what you're willing to potentially let go of to get it. Love requires sacrifice, and if you aren't willing to do what you need to in order to get it, you won't find it."

"So you aren't going to give me the answers?"

"Of course not. Because I don't have them. I can only put you on the path, and then I have to let you make your own decisions. But whatever your decision, make it a good one." She looked toward the compound. "You have done well. Your family is healthy and happy, and you have a little one on the way very soon."

"Mikael...."

"I am well aware of my Supreme Alpha's actions, but don't be so quick to give credit to others. You lead and care about your family. That's what's most important. And as for your mate...." She began to fade, the light growing dimmer until he was surrounded by darkness.

"Dang it. Always knows how to make a great exit."

Laughter filled the night and then faded away.

Tobias stood alone, then shifted back to his wolf form and walked slowly back to the compound.

"What's going on?" Ryan asked as he came out of his cabin, blinking but alert. "Is everything all right?"

"It's nothing." Tobias wanted Ryan to relax. The day had been exciting enough, and everyone needed rest and some quiet time. They were creatures of nature, and her cycles and all the activity was going to overwhelm them. They lived their lives close to the land and the changing seasons, away from intense daily drama. "I couldn't sleep and decided to take a run."

"Out to the creek? Isn't that a little dangerous at this time of night? There's that cougar, and Zev is around somewhere."

"I can take care of myself, Ryan." Tobias wasn't sure if that was for himself or his beta. The truth was, Zev had gotten the better of him, and he was wondering if he was strong enough to lead this pack. The expression of doubt on Ryan's face only reinforced that. "I'm going back up to bed." He turned away and went inside.

"Where were you?' Pete asked when he returned to the bedroom. Tobias stripped down and got back into bed. "You smell like flowers and fresh air."

"I went for a run."

Pete sniffed. "No. You did something else. When you go for a run, you smell like pine and woods. That's what you smelled like this morning. This is different, and I doubt you went to the glade." Pete leaned closer once again. "It's very nice."

"I was at the creek." Tobias didn't feel comfortable talking about what he'd seen. He felt that was between him and the goddess.

Pete pushed the covers away and straddled his hips, pressing his hands to Tobias's chest. "Do you have condoms?"

"We don't need any. Human diseases don't pass to us, and I can't pass anything to you." Tobias slid his hands up Pete's belly to his shoulders, then tugged him down to meet him. "I want to be inside you bare, to feel you with nothing between us. I want to hear you scream and yell as I make you forget your name."

Pete kissed him hard, vibrating with excitement. When they broke the kiss, he straightened. Tobias watched intently as Pete rolled his hips, sliding up and back along his cock, which throbbed and ached something terrible. He wanted Pete so badly. His wolf screamed and howled for it, and it was all he could do to keep the animal part of his nature at bay.

Tobias slid his hands along Pete's thighs. He lifted him and brought Pete closer until he was right there. Tobias needed a taste, and he took it, plunging his lips down Pete's cock. The air whooshed from Pete's lungs in a more than gratifying sound. Pete was salty, musky, and absolutely delicious. He was his mate, and that meant he was perfect for him.

"Tobias…."

He didn't stop and loved Pete's whine and the small gasps for breath. Tobias sucked and laved along Pete's length, holding him steady, buttcheeks in his large hands, keeping Pete exactly where he wanted him

"Is everyone asleep?" They were back to Pete's worry.

Tobias sucked harder. Pete groaned, and it didn't matter if they weren't asleep—they were going to listen to his Pete making a symphony of sound. He pulled off, saying, "Sweetheart, you're beautiful, and there's nothing to be shy about." He held still, gazing at Pete, then set Pete on the bed beside him, bounced up, and pressed Pete facedown into the mattress.

Tobias stalked up him, hands leading the way until they slid over Pete's bubble butt and spread the cheeks to expose the center of him. As Tobias leaned in, the muscles pulsed, smelling of his mate, only stronger.

"What are you doing?" Pete gasped.

"I'm making you mine." It was the only answer he had. At this moment, this was as close as he dared get to mating Pete. He wanted him badly. His wolf screamed for him to bury himself inside Pete, kiss, lick, and bite him to make him his forever. Tobias licked up Pete's crease and then probed his puckered hole and teased as Pete went to pieces around him. Musk, earth, and the sweetness that was Pete burst on his tongue. "Has anyone ever done this for you?"

"No...." The word came out shaky.

"Then they don't know what they're missing." He delved deep, letting his mate surround him. He needed to remember everything about Pete—the way he smelled, sounded, and tasted.

Pete quivered, the entire bed shaking, as he moaned and mewled deeply. Those sounds drove Tobias's wolf to the fore. His mate wanted him, and there was nothing he wanted more than to have him.

Tobias backed away, clearing his clouded head, and then grabbed the lube, slicking himself, then moved into position. He licked at the back of Pete's neck. The blood coursed through Pete, calling to Tobias like a siren song. As he sank inside his mate, Tobias arched his back, then held still. He didn't want to hurt, but all his instincts urged him to take what was his.

Pete gasped and then groaned as Tobias sank deeper and deeper. The heat, the pressure around him, was all exquisite and amazing. His mate was an incredible man, and not just because of how Tobias felt at this very moment. Everything about him spoke to Tobias—the way he smelled, like the forest after a rain; the way he tasted, hot, spicy, earthy; the way he felt, even hotter, volcanic....

"Are you going to move?" Pete pressed back, pushing into Tobias. "Stop woolgathering and fuck me." He rocked his hips, stealing the air from Tobias's lungs.

He pressed Pete to the mattress, held him still, and then snapped his hips. Pete moaned and gasped, and arched his back until Tobias was able to meet his lips in a sloppy kiss. God, he wanted, and Pete gave without hesitation. It was like he knew what Tobias needed. "I don't… want to… hurt you."

"I'm not made of glass." Pete squirmed forward off him and rolled over. He wound his legs around Tobias's hips, and Tobias slid back inside him with a long growl of pleasure. "Now fuck me like you mean it."

Tobias pulled out and drove back into his mate.

"Yes… yes… yes!" Pete held him by the neck, tugging him closer. "God, right there and don't you dare stop."

For a second Tobias wondered what had happened to the quiet man worried about the others hearing what was happening. "Gonna fuck you into the middle of next week. You're mine, and I'm going to show you. Want you to feel me forever." He snapped his hips, slapping against Pete's ass. With each thrust, his passion grew, and the control on his wolf slipped further away. A full-throated growl escaped, and Tobias saw Pete in black-and-white. His gums ached as his teeth extended. He was shifting, and that meant a loss of control. Tobias pushed it back, watching Pete as he writhed under him.

"Don't you dare stop!" Pete gripped the side of Tobias's head and kissed him hard.

Tobias tasted blood and stopped all movement, physically and mentally forcing his wolf to recede. He was seconds from losing all control and mating Pete against his will. He licked his lips, the coppery taste of Pete's blood bursting on his tongue. He wanted more, to have him forever, for Pete to be his. But he'd made a promise, and even though the Mother had confirmed that Pete was his mate, he wasn't going to take him against his will.

"What's going on?" Pete grabbed his hips and pulled him forward.

Tobias wasn't in a position to talk, so he concentrated on control and gave Pete what they both needed so badly.

With Pete writhing on the bed and moaning at the top of his lungs, it wasn't long before he pulled Tobias to the edge. Normally he'd try to wait, but his control was so tenuous, he tumbled over, gazing deeply into Pete's eyes. "You're amazing."

He withdrew and lay on the bed, his head swimming. But there was no time for afterglow. Pete was wanting—he could hear it in the way Pete's blood coursed through him. He held Pete close and licked the sweat off his chest and belly, before swallowing his cock to the root.

Pete went wild, bucking up, but Tobias was determined to get a good taste of his mate. Using his tongue, he swirled it around the head until Pete whimpered. He was on the edge, and Tobias sucked harder until Pete spilled, crying out at the top of his lungs, as Tobias swallowed all his mate had to give.

Pete stilled, and Tobias let his softening cock slip from between his lips. "I feel so alive right now."

Tobias understood that. He'd been in a haze of sorts and was coming into the light of day. Too bad that light was on a timer.

TOBIAS GOT up as usual and did his rounds, making sure everything and everyone was safe and secure. When he came back inside, his mother was waiting for him in her robe and passed him a mug of coffee.

"I'm not as young as I used to be and I know I'm your mother, but I've seen more than most people have a right to."

He knew she was winding up to something. "What are you getting at?"

"I know how your father would feel if what happened to you had happened to him."

"Mom...."

Pete came out in a T-shirt and shorts and sat next to him. "Listen to your mother."

Tobias growled. "I'm being ganged up on."

"No. You are being talked to by your mother." She sat across from him. "I know what that did to you. Your pride is finding it hard to take that Zev got the better of you. But remember that he did it with subterfuge and craft."

"He laid traps and worked silver into the rope," Pete said.

"Exactly." His mother agreeing with Pete was both worrying and comforting. "He planned this, and he planned for you to die in the fire, and he wanted to burn us all out. Have no doubt about that."

"But I should have been smart enough to see that and—"

"No. You have good people who surround you, and someone who cared enough about you to be concerned and to try to find you."

Tobias took Pete's hand under the table. He really was thankful for what he'd done.

"Your brother wasn't counting on that. It's his weakness and your strength."

"I know he hurts you, Mom. That you wish he was different."

"Yes. I've wondered what I did wrong but have come to the conclusion that Zev made his own decisions and there is nothing I can do about them." She sipped from her mug. "But we got off track. What I truly wanted to say is that you can't control everything, and that what Zev did to you is not a reflection on you or how you lead this pack."

"But…."

"No. I mean it. I know you spent much of last night with a bruised ego, as well as a battered body. And you need to get past it fast. The pack needs you just as much today as they did two days ago. A lot has happened, and you need to be steady and strong. Zev has attacked the pack, tried to burn us out, and he's gone after Pete here, a guest and someone under our protection. Keep strong and vigilant for him and for all of us."

"So I'm supposed to just put what happened behind me?"

"You're damn right. Learn from it and move on. Dwelling on it and letting it eat at you does no good at all." She put her mug down, though she kept her hands around it. "After your father was killed, I had to get you three kids to safety and do the best I could for all of you. I missed your father very much, but I had to go on for you, and you need to do the same for them."

"But how can I protect them from Zev when I couldn't even protect myself from him?"

"That's your ego talking, and you need to give it a rest." His mother could be just as stubborn as he could sometimes. "This isn't about you, but all of us, and there isn't a single person out there who feels that anyone else would make a better leader."

Tobias sighed.

"If it makes you feel better, talk to Alpha Mikael, but I'm sure he'd tell you the same things we are."

That didn't sit any better than anything else did at the moment. Tobias hated feeling this unsettled. He had spent so much of his life without a real pack that felt like home—that had been taken away after his dad's death—and he was afraid history would repeat itself. He couldn't lose his family again. "I just need a chance to work through this on my own."

"If you say so, but I somehow doubt you're going to get it."

Was there something his mother knew that he didn't?

"Let's go get dressed and I'll help your mom make breakfast," Pete said, standing.

"Okay. I'm going to check with Greg and the guys to verify that our borders are safe for now." He hurried back to his room to get dressed and then left the house as fast as he could. He really needed a chance to think and work through what had happened. Yes, he knew he was the victim of an attack, by his own half brother. Tobias felt helpless, though he knew he wasn't. He was strong, but strength wasn't everything. He had to be smart.

"Everything was quiet," Greg told him. "I ran most of the night, keeping an eye on our borders, and there were no incursions as far as I can tell."

"You didn't smell him at all?"

"It's hard to tell near where the fire was because the scorched earth is so powerful, but I could tell where I think he was singed and which way he went by faint tracks. I don't think he's been back, and he was hurt pretty badly. Are you all right?"

"Yes. Thank you."

Greg shifted his gaze to the ground. "We were all worried."

"I know. Mom and Pete took good care of me and I got some rest." He kept his gaze steady because this whole situation wasn't something he wanted to talk about.

"You're a good alpha and I want you to stay." Greg turned and hurried away.

Tobias watched him go and then walked toward the pack house. Pete stood outside the door, watching him, arms folded, an "I told you so" expression on his adorable features. Well, at the moment they weren't quite so cute. Then he went inside, and Tobias continued making his rounds. He was very unsettled and it wasn't going away.

"Alpha!" Sasha called more sharply than usual. "It's Lorraine. I think she's going into labor, for real this time."

"Okay. I'll get Mom." Tobias strode across the compound as a yell cut the quiet morning.

His mother met him at the door as he approached. "I'm on my way." She breezed by him, and Elayne was already walking toward the cabin.

As Tobias stepped inside, Pete called, "What's all the commotion?" He seemed to have taken over the kitchen. "Your mother left like she was on fire."

"Lorraine is having her baby. It's early, and I think all the excitement hasn't been good for her. Lorraine comes off as a ballbuster, but this is her first child and I think she's overdone it the last few days…. She's as stubborn as any of us and won't listen no matter what."

"Is there anything I can do?"

"Just what you're doing. We'll have to take food over to them. The women are trying to help her." Tobias hoped like hell there were no complications for her. The hospitals weren't nearby. Usually their births were simpler and less complicated than human births, but he knew anything was possible. "Mom has had plenty of experience." He was wondering if he was trying to comfort Pete or himself.

Pete returned his attention to the stove. "Can I make a suggestion?"

"You can say anything."

"Have the men you can spare on alert. If your mom and Elayne knew Lorraine needed them, then if Zev is anywhere around here, he's going to hear all of this as well. He's going to know that a lot of the pack's attention will be on her, so he may try to take advantage."

"I was hoping we could go swimming or something this afternoon." It was their last day together and he wanted to make it special. Instead the drama of the last two days was going to continue. Not that he could blame Lorraine or anyone else. Things were just conspiring against them at the moment.

Tobias had spent hours running through his options, and more than once had come close to telling Pete they were mates. But nothing had changed and he wasn't going to take Pete's choices away from him.

"We'll get some time alone. I'll do my best to help with that. But you need to make sure your sister is okay and that we're safe." Pete continued to work at the stove. "I have this and I'll make up plates for everyone. Just have them come in to eat when they can, and I'll get things together for the ladies."

"You are so amazing." Tobias kissed him, heard Lorraine cry out once again, and raced across to the new cabin. He went inside, where his mother sat with Lorraine, whose eyes were wild and was sweating like she'd run a marathon. Tobias approached her and placed one hand on her forehead and the other on her belly.

Lorraine's breathing relaxed and she actually smiled.

"It will be okay. He's settling down now." Tobias met her gaze for a few minutes, doing his best to convey peace and care. "You need to rest."

"Are you sure it's a boy?" Lorraine asked.

"Yes. And he's strong," Tobias said, comforting her. "Just let it come. Don't try to stop it. He's ready to meet the world."

"But I thought it was too soon."

"It's fine." Tobias kissed her on the forehead and then left her and the women alone. He didn't need to be in the way. Women had been having babies for as long as the human race was on earth, and wolves, his family, had been having them here, where the goddess was close and could watch over them, for just as long.

Outside, he met with the men and told them his thoughts. "We need to find where Zev is staying and figure out what he has planned next. I'm getting very tired of being at his mercy."

Brick nodded. "Greg and I are good trackers. We'll follow his scent from last night if we can and see where it leads."

"Don't enter the territory of any other packs but find him."

They nodded and headed toward the edge of the settlement, then stripped off their jeans and shirts before shifting and disappearing into the trees.

Tobias turned to Ryan. "You and I need to keep the settlement safe. Patrol the area and watch for any sign of Zev."

"We're spread very thin right now."

"I know." Tobias bit his lower lip. Goddess, he hated this.

"A good leader knows when he needs to ask for help." Ryan clapped his shoulder in a show of support.

Tobias nodded. "I'm going to contact Mikael and see if he can help us." He had no choice. Swallowing his pride for a few days was worth keeping his pack safe. He turned and went inside and sent Mikael an e-mail and received the near-instant response that he'd send his enforcer, Katherine, and two other wolves to help. They'd be leaving in less than an hour.

Pete had food ready, and Tobias ate while Pete took some out to the women. He didn't come back right away, but when he did, he was grinning. "You're an uncle. She named him Edward after your father." Pete took his empty plate. "He's a cute little peanut, and both he and your sister are doing just fine."

"That's good news."

"Go on and see them. Your mother and Elayne are eating, and they have a plate for Lorraine. It's all good." Pete blinked, fighting tears. "She let me hold him and asked if I wanted to be Uncle Pete." A tear escaped and ran down his face. "I never expected to be uncle to anyone… ever. I don't know what changed her mind about me, but…."

"You changed her mind. No one else."

"I wonder what I did?" Pete asked and busied himself in the kitchen.

Ryan came inside, and Pete got him a heaping plate of pancakes. He took it outside, leaving them alone once again.

"You were yourself. That's all. You've been kind and caring the entire time you've been here. Why do you think everyone thinks well of you?" Tobias was seconds from begging Pete to stay with him. But what the hell good would that do? Yes, he wanted Pete more than he'd wanted anything else in his life. But Pete deserved to make his own decisions, and that was more important than anything else. Tobias had seen Anton take away the choices of others, and he was never going to do that. "You know there would always be a place here with us if you wanted it."

Pete didn't turn around, but Tobias heard the roughness in his voice. "Thank you. I appreciate that so much. But I don't belong here. Everyone has something they're good at, that they can contribute to the group. I don't have that. I'd be a drain on everyone here, and...." Pete slowly turned and stepped close. "I know I care for you. Very much. But I have a life back in New York. I have friends, and I'm trying to make my way. It's what I know and understand, Tobias. I'm not part of what you have here. We've been through a lot in the last few days, and I'm very grateful for everything you've done for me."

"I'm glad you've been here."

"It has never been boring. That's for sure. But I think you need to meet someone like you, who understands all this and what's expected of them. You and your family have a great life here, but as much as I want... as I hope I might.... Tobias, I don't know." He closed his eyes, and Tobias hugged him close. "It's nice here and I feel like I could belong, but I don't understand how that's possible. I've only been here for a few days and I'm happy."

That set Tobias's heart racing, and his wolf pranced and thumped his tail. "This is very different from what you're used to, but if you stayed—" He didn't get a chance to finish his sentence.

"Why? I'd only be a burden to you and the rest of the pack." Pete put his arms around Tobias's waist and held him. "How long do you think our relationship would last when you found out that I can't do shit? I can cook and pick up stuff around here. I don't have any survival skills. Not really. I got lucky the night I managed to stumble into your barn. There's no other explanation." Pete buried his face in Tobias's shirt. "You deserve someone better than me, someone who can be a part of your life."

"What if you're the one I want?"

"It doesn't matter. People like me for a while, but most of them figure out I'm not worth much and they leave or send me away. I need some stability." When Pete grew silent, Tobias held him tighter. Pete kept his face buried against Tobias's shirt, and he thought Pete was crying. He held Pete tighter and let him get out what was bothering him. Abruptly Pete pulled back, turned away, and returned to work. "You'll find someone else, someone better for you than a kid who doesn't know shit and isn't worth it anyway."

Tobias wondered where this was coming from. His instincts told him it was so much more than the thought of leaving. Before he could argue, Pete continued.

"You should go see your nephew and welcome him into the pack. I'm assuming you have something special that you do." Pete wiped his eyes. "Just leave me for a while and let me wallow in my misery while you're gone. I'll be okay in a little bit." He guided Tobias toward the door. It has been years since someone had last guided him anywhere or pushed him around, and here his little mate was giving him the bum's rush.

"Why are you doing this?" Tobias asked, stopping Pete.

"Look. I'm an orphan, and I've spent so much of my life on my own, I don't know any other way. But now I've made some close friends, like Roger, and I can't give them up... can't let go of everything and stay here." He wiped his eyes once again. "I'm drawn to you, and you have been so good to me. Your offer is so unexpected and kind, I can't tell you how much it...." Pete put his hand over his heart and turned away again. "Just go and see your nephew, please."

"I don't want to leave you while you're feeling this way."

Pete turned back around. "You know, you aren't the only one with an ego, and I don't want you to see me if I go to pieces, okay?"

Tobias sighed and left the house to do as Pete wanted.

Lorraine was in bed, holding her baby to her, as proud and tired as any new mother he'd ever seen. He touched her forehead lightly and then sat on the edge of the bed. "Can I see the newest member of our pack?"

She slowly handed him over. Little Edward's eyes opened, and the two of them shared their first gaze.

"You are going to be a great wolf, you know that? Maybe someday you'll be the one to take over from me." He had ice-blue eyes as intense as any Tobias had ever seen. "I'm your alpha, and when you get older, your daddy, mommy, and I will show you how to hunt and run, and play in the creek. You're going to be a strong wolf, and I promise that I'll show you how to shift when the time comes."

Edward yawned and closed his eyes once again. His lips moved like he was looking for food.

"Yeah, you're a member of this family," Tobias chuckled. He took Edward to the door of the cabin and stepped outside, shielding his eyes from the light. "Mother, goddess and guardian of us all. I present to you my nephew, Edward. He is the newest member of our pack, and I promise we shall raise him to know, respect, and love you as we all do."

A light breeze swirled around the two of them, like they were being caressed, and then died away.

Edward fussed, so Tobias took him back inside and gently laid him with his mother. "Rest, Lorraine. If you need anything, let Elayne or Mom know. Pete is manning the kitchen for now."

"Mom is lying down somewhere." Lorraine twisted so she could feed Edward. "So have you told Pete what he is to you?"

"No. I'm taking him back tomorrow."

She groaned. "Sometimes I wonder if you have the brains the Mother gave an ant. He's your mate and you can't let him go. Pete is the only mate you will ever have." Her eyes blazed and then gentled when she looked at Edward. "I don't know what I'd do if I didn't have Sasha. I know I can be a real bitch, but he understands and brings out the best of me. I can't imagine my life without him." She closed her eyes and relaxed back on the pillow. "Think about your life and how it's going to look in ten years."

"This isn't going to help, because I won't trap him here. I know Pete. He's one of those people who would do just about anything to make others happy. I know that in my heart, and if he thought it would make me happy for him to stay with me, then he would, regardless of what he wanted. I can't do that. So I have to let him go."

"And give up the other half of your soul? Some wolves look their entire lives and never find their mate. You were lucky enough to have him wander into your life, and you're going to let him leave?" Lorraine glared at him. "If I wasn't holding my baby, I'd smack some sense into you, alpha or not."

"It's the way things are."

"The goddess doesn't give us what we don't need."

"I know. That's what she said last night." Tobias waited for Lorraine's reaction, and he wasn't disappointed by her impression of a big-mouth bass. "She told me that it was never wise to ignore her gifts, but she also said that I had to follow my heart and do what I thought was best. She really was less than helpful, but I appreciate that she'll let me decide."

"You saw the Mother? Last night? Were you drunk, or did you get into some wolfsbane?"

"No. She was at the creek waiting for me. I'm not going to go into anything else." He was still awed that she appeared to him.

"Fine. But whatever you decide, don't mess this up. You work hard to make all of us happy—don't walk away from the chance to be happy yourself." She covered up her chest as Edward fell asleep. "Is it okay if I rest for a while? If he's asleep, I need to try to do the same."

"We'll bring you something to eat in a few hours." Tobias stood. "Rest." Then he listened. "Where's Sasha?"

"He's with Ryan, patrolling. I told him if he kept hovering over me, I was going to go crazy."

"I understand." Tobias left her and the baby and returned to the pack house as the help they needed arrived. "Katherine." Tobias had met her on a few occasions. As another strong wolf, the two of them usually circled one other to get their measure, but not this time.

"Alpha, what do you need? Mikael said you were having trouble with one of Anton's children." She took in their surroundings, as alert as any wolf he'd ever seen.

"He's my half brother. My mother was with Anton before she escaped from his pack. Then she met her mate, my father. Zev and I grew up together, but we are nothing alike. It's hard to believe we have the same mother."

Someone cleared their throat behind Katherine, and she actually looked contrite. "I'm sorry."

"My sister forgets her manners. I'm Christopher, and this is my mate, Fredrick. He is also one of Anton's children. He might be able to shed some light. What do you need from us?"

Tobias shook hands with both men. "Zev has attacked me personally...." Goddess, that was so hard to admit, but they needed to know the truth. "He also tried to burn us out. Zev is older than I am and feels that he should be alpha of this pack. He challenged me shortly after I was made alpha, but he lost."

"You didn't kill him?" Katherine asked dispassionately.

"No. I banished him, for our mom's sake, and we heard nothing from him until earlier this week."

Both Katherine and Fredrick nodded. "I'm willing to bet he was biding his time and building his strength. When he challenged you, he wasn't strong enough to defeat you, but that's not the case now." Fredrick stepped in front of the others. The hatred and intensity that Zev always had was missing from Fredrick, who was calm and almost serene. There was power behind his eyes, but at the same time, a gentleness that made him unthreatening. "One thing my father had was an abundance of intelligence. He used it for ill and let the darkness take over, but that doesn't mean he wasn't vindictive as hell. How long was your brother under my father's thumb?"

"He was four, I think, when Mom escaped."

Fredrick groaned. "You said you didn't know where he's been until he showed up. I'm willing to bet he reconnected with my fucked-up family."

"But Mikael defeated Anton."

"And I defeated my brother, but that doesn't mean the poison my father cultivated and spread for years isn't still out there. Turn over a rock where my family has been and the filth will bubble up." A truck pulled up and two additional wolves climbed out. "That's Kaiawa and Stephan."

Tobias shook hands with both of them. Kaiawa was tall, strong, and of Native American heritage, while Stephan was a little smaller.

"Kaiawa is one of Mikael and Denton's betas," Katherine explained as she took control of the conversation. "Stephan—"

"I managed to get away from Fredrick's brother." He seemed a little jumpy and stayed close to Kaiawa. Tobias wondered what was up with them. He scented, and they weren't mated, but the attraction between them was palpable.

"I have two wolves out at the moment, trying to track Zev. We have no idea what he's planning next, but we've stopped him so far."

"He'll most likely escalate," Fredrick explained, and the others nodded their agreement. "Katherine, Christopher, Kaiawa, and Stephan are here to help with any manpower you need, but I spent my entire life under Anton and then my brother, so I came to explain some of the underlying factors you're dealing with."

"When do you expect your men back?" Katherine asked.

"They're very good trackers and amazing at not being seen and keeping downwind. Brick and Greg will stay on what I assigned them until they're successful."

"Okay. Then in the meantime, we'll patrol the area and try to identify specific lines of attack. We'll also set some traps, and I'll explain what we've set and give you exact locations when we're done. The one way to bring this to an end is to capture or kill Zev. If my people or I discover him, there will no mercy. Not everyone is like Fredrick here." She nodded toward Fredrick with respect.

"Thank you for your help. All of you."

"We are all one pack," Kaiawa said, showing his neck, and the others followed suit. There wasn't going to be a threat to Tobias's authority from any of them. "Mikael believes that we need to help one another. Spend less time fighting for our place in the hierarchy and more time working together."

"My father was able to rise to power by using the fact that all the packs were independent against them," Fredrick noted.

Katherine nodded. "We should get to work. I'm going to take the three of them, and we'll get the lay of the land. Call when your men return."

"We don't have much room...." Tobias had been wondering where he was going to put everyone up.

"We'll spend the night out there. Don't worry about us. Mikael asked us to stay for as long as necessary." She motioned toward the trees, and everyone but Fredrick followed her. They stripped and shifted at the edge of the forest and disappeared.

"You have nothing to worry about with Katherine, or any of us. We truly want to help. My family has caused enough havoc over the past few years that we've all had enough."

"Why didn't you turn out like the rest of them?"

"My mother. She showed me love and kept telling me that no matter what, there was a better way than what my family did. Mom tried to help my brother Juneau, but he'd have none of it. He was too close to my father and idolized him. The end came when my father sent me to college because he thought I could help the pack and him. It turned out I was able to get away from him and his influence."

"How did you do that?" Tobias asked as he motioned toward the door and followed Fredrick inside. Most wolves thought he was being gracious, but he followed people so they couldn't make a move behind his back. Zev, and others like him, had no sense of fair play at all.

"I listened to my mother."

Tobias stepped inside. He didn't hear Pete and sniffed. He wasn't there, and a hint of worry spiked his belly. It took a second for him to pull his attention back to Fredrick.

"I've come to understand that some of my family members have an elemental connection. Mine and my brother's is to air. My father's was fire, and I suspect Zev's is as well. My mother told me never to use it, that it was dark. She got that impression from my father. But it isn't. The power is just that—power. It isn't good or bad. It just is."

"Where did you learn that?" Tobias got some grape juice from the refrigerator, poured two glasses, and offered one to Fredrick.

"It's a long story, but the Mother was the one who led me to understanding."

"She has a way of doing that." Tobias drank in a gulp and set the glass down. He peered out the window, hoping to see Pete. God, he hoped he hadn't decided to go out with Katherine and the others, though that wasn't likely. "So what can you tell me?"

"If he's using his power, it will drain him. He can't continue to do so without it taking a physical toll. The last time I used it to help the Mother, I spent all the energy I had, and it took days before I felt like myself again. But it also plays with the mind. Using the power makes you feel invincible and then you think it's the answer to everything. I haven't tapped into that part of myself since, and I'll be happy if I never have to again."

"All right. How do we use his own power against him?"

"I'll have to think on it. My brother was able to take a normal storm and enhance it to threatening proportions. Because I have power over the same element and I was stronger than him, I turned the storm back on its creator. I don't know another fire elemental…."

"But you could control his fire with wind."

"Or fan the flames to blast-furnace heat. I don't have a lot of experience, but if he does attack, I'll do my best. I need my mate with me, though. Christopher helps ground me and gives me the control I need."

Checking out the window yet again, Tobias finally saw Pete, coming out of the new cabin. He smiled as he crossed the compound and joined them inside. Tobias made introductions, and Fredrick greeted Pete suspiciously.

"You have nothing to fear from me. I'm only here until tomorrow, and I've already promised Tobias I will keep your secret." Pete sat and put his feet up. "I'm so tired. I don't usually get up this early, and I've been feeding everyone and helping with the baby. He's such a little sweetheart. Lorraine is doing well, but she needs sleep, and Edward needs to be fed every few hours. I got her to express some milk, and I just got done feeding him so she could rest." Pete turned and smiled. "You know, your sister is quite a lady. Especially when she's asleep."

Tobias laughed. "You certainly have her number." His sister could definitely be a pain in the rear.

"Lorraine isn't that bad. She's just tired, and she's been carrying a baby around with her for months." Pete closed his eyes and then snapped them open, slapping his hand over his mouth. "I'm sorry. You were talking and I came right in and just took over." He jumped to his feet. "I'll go find something else to do." He was about to leave the room, but Tobias caught his arm and guided Pete onto his lap.

"Fredrick and I were just talking for a few minutes. He and some of his pack members are helping us out for a few days until we can catch up with Zev." He held Pete tight. "Do you know where my mother and Elayne are?"

"Clarie is lying down for a little while, and Elayne was busy taking care of all the laundry from the birth."

Tobias cocked his ears and listened. He could have sworn....

"What is it?" Pete asked as he snuggled closer.

"I heard it too." Fredrick was already on his feet. "That's a cry for help."

Pete jumped up, with Tobias right behind him.

"Fredrick, stay here with Pete and get everyone, including my sister and the baby, in here. Wake my mother, and once everyone is safe, bolt the doors." Tobias raced outside, yanked his clothes off, shifted, and bolted for the woods as fast as his wolf legs would carry him.

He pounded the ground, listening to every sound. The scent of his half brother was strong on the air. The pained cry for help grew louder, and he smelled other wolves in the area, converging, scents strengthening on the wind.

Small animals scurried out of his way as he continued as fast as possible. Tobias stopped as he got close. Zev's scent was fading, which was both a relief and a worry. Where was he heading? Tobias cautiously stepped forward.

Sasha lay on his side, trying to get up, his foot in a trap.

Tobias shifted as other wolves arrived. "Watch where you step. If there's one trap, there will be more." Barefoot, he grabbed a stick, testing the ground before stepping.

The stick snapped loudly as a trap closed with bone-crushing force. He grabbed the spring trap, pulled the stake it was attached to out of the ground, and tossed it aside. Then he continued forward, reached Sasha, and freed his injured foot. "You need to shift for me. It's the only way you can heal."

"I don't think he can right now." Katherine examined the trap and hissed, snapping back. "There's silver on the teeth, the bastard."

Tobias gently lifted Sasha into his arms as Katherine stood.

"Let me carry him."

He nodded and passed Sasha to her, and she cradled him gently. This woman was one hell of a dichotomy. Tobias would have liked to think on that for a few seconds, but fear spiked in the back of his head, blooming like pain and spreading through him. Tobias looked around. Everyone was alert but relatively calm. "It's Pete! Get back to the compound. Something is going on!"

Brick, Greg, and Christopher shifted immediately and took off through the woods. Kaiawa and Stephan did the same, following behind by only a few seconds.

"You need to go with them. I have him." Katherine was already moving quickly through the forest.

"Call if you need anything." Tobias was torn, but Katherine was more than capable, so he shifted and sped away.

The forest floor flew by under his feet, which barely touched the ground. He caught up to the others, passed them, and barreled into the empty compound. He stopped, scenting the air. He smelled the pack in the house, but no Zev. That was good. The spike of fear seemed to have passed, and he reached the cabin, shifted, and burst inside, naked.

"What's wrong?" He glared at all of them. Pete sat on the sofa with Tobias's nephew in his arms. "Where's Lorraine?"

"She's lying down. We got everyone in here and she started to bleed a little," his mother said calmly. "She's fine, but she needs to sleep."

"I put her in the room I've been using." Pete stood and took the baby down the hall. He returned with his arms empty. "You're naked," he whispered.

Tobias left the cabin to get his clothes. The others were arriving, and he explained what had happened. They hurried to get dressed, and then Greg and Brick returned to see if Katherine needed any help.

"Is he your mate?" Kaiawa asked, and sniffed him. "You haven't completed the bond."

Tobias hardened his expression, and Kaiawa backed away, mumbling a quick apology. "It's something I don't want to discuss."

Kaiawa nodded, and Katherine entered the compound, still carrying Sasha.

"He's becoming more alert." She set him down, and Tobias gently stroked Sasha's coat.

"You need to shift. Remember your pup. He needs you to shift." Tobias stepped back, and slowly Sasha's form elongated. It was a long process, but in the end, he was in human form and his leg was whole. Tobias felt it to make sure the bone had knitted together. "You're going to be all right."

"Thank you, alpha." Sasha slowly got to his feet, and Christopher handed Sasha his clothes.

"Get dressed. Your mate is in the pack house, sleeping. She's going to be very happy to see you." Tobias patted him on the shoulder, and Sasha pulled on his clothes and went inside. "Do you know if Brick and Greg were able to find where Zev is staying?" Tobias asked Katherine.

"No. I'm going to dress, and then we'll see what we can find out." Her face contorted with anger, her eyes burning. "He has to be stopped. This kind of behavior is…." Her hands clenched into fists.

"I agree. Please see what you can find out. Getting inside his head is turning out to be impossible. I used to think I knew him, but Zev isn't the man I grew up with." Tobias felt very helpless and he hated it. He was an alpha, and it was his job to have answers and know what direction to take. "Let's see if there's something to eat." He led her inside, where his mother and Pete were making sandwiches and passing them out.

"What about Brick and Greg? I haven't seen them."

"They'll hunt for what they need." Tobias hugged Pete to him, let his scent surround him, and almost instantly, some of the doubts slipped away. "Are you really okay? I felt your distress."

Pete lifted his gaze. "How is that possible? I was afraid for Lorraine. She was bleeding pretty badly and I panicked for a second."

His mate was amazing. His own fear spiked because of what was happening to Tobias's sister, the one person in the pack who had been less than welcoming to him. Pete had an amazing heart, and already a sense of loss washed over Tobias.

"We found a silver-laced trap, and there may be others. Do you think you can help me dispose of that one and look for others?" The silver wouldn't bother Pete the way it would the rest of the pack.

"Sure. I still need to get rid of the blanket too," Pete said, always so willing and eager to help.

Today was his last day with Pete. Tomorrow he'd promised to take him to meet his group for his flight home. He tried not to think about it too hard. He needed to make the most of the time they had together, no matter what they were doing. This was his decision and he was prepared to live with it. At least he hoped to hell he was.

CHAPTER 7

PETE KNEW there was something Tobias wasn't telling him. He searched his expression, but Tobias had been closed off since they'd returned from the woods. They'd found a total of three traps that they'd put into heavy bags, and Tobias said he'd dispose of them.

Pete went to the kitchen where Clarie was making more sandwiches. The day had already been way too busy, and he hoped it quieted down. Granted, the last few days had been a hive of activity. And Pete thought New York was fast-paced.

"Go spend some time with Tobias. I have this." Clarie was an incredible lady. She made up two plates and handed them to him. Of course, the one for Tobias had three sandwiches on it, while his had one.

"Let's go outside," Tobias offered, and Pete nodded. There were too many people in the house, and Pete wanted some time with Tobias but thought he might have too much going on. Tobias held the door for him, and they sat at a crude picnic table in the shade of one of the trees.

"I'm sorry about all of this," Tobias said once they had begun eating. "I'd hoped we'd have some time alone together."

"You've barely had a chance to take a breath." Maybe this was all for the best. Pete had engaged his heart without really thinking too much about the consequences.

Tobias stood, came around to the same side of the table as him, and sat right next to him. "I know. I blame my brother for that." Tobias held him close, and Pete thought he might have been rubbing him. He liked when Tobias held him, but Tobias should be eating his lunch, not licking and….

Pete groaned when Tobias found that spot at the base of his neck, worrying it with his tongue. He was instantly hard, and Tobias cupped him through his pants.

"Tobias, I…." Pete closed his eyes as Tobias rubbed harder, then popped the buttons on his pants and slid his fingers inside.

"That's it." Tobias's gravelly, deep voice rang in Pete's ears and thrummed in his gut. Tobias ran his thumb over the head of his cock, and Pete shook, holding on to Tobias so he didn't fly apart.

"How can you do that?" He felt like a fucking teenager who'd just discovered his own dick. All Tobias had to do was touch him and he was right there, instantly on edge, aching to come.

"Because I'm good." Tobias sucked Pete's ear, and Pete groaned.

"You can't do this. What if someone comes out?"

"They won't," he said a little louder and gripped Pete tighter as he pressed him back. He cradled Pete in his arms and laid him back on the bench. Tobias parted his pants and pulled out his dick.

Pete whimpered as Tobias stroked him, hovering over him. Tobias's eyes blazed. "God!"

"I know exactly how close you are, and I want you to stay right there." Tobias gripped him but didn't move. Pete's cock throbbed. He needed more sensation, more… something… anything. "That's it. Are you on the edge?"

"Yeah." Pete clamped his eyes closed and immediately missed seeing Tobias's. Sliding them open, he groaned at the intense passion glowing at him.

"I know you're leaving, but I can't let you go without telling you that I love you." Tobias stroked him hard and fast, stopped, and then leaned down and engulfed him in his heated mouth. Pete cried out, shaking as the pressure built. Tobias bobbed his head, sucking him hard, and Pete nearly came apart, but he held off.

Tobias slid his hand under Pete's shirt, heat spreading where he touched. Pete groaned and then whimpered when Tobias found his nipple and pinched it just so. That sent him over the edge, and Pete shouted his pleasure to the trees and sky, completely falling apart as he came down Tobias's throat. He closed his eyes, held still, and breathed deeply as Tobias licked him clean and then slowly withdrew his lips.

"I want to remember you." Tobias moved away and carefully straightened Pete's clothes, with such gentleness and care. "And I want you to remember me."

"How could I forget?" Pete sat up, a little dizzy but happy, and put his arms around Tobias's neck. "I really wish things had been different and that…." He couldn't finish through the ache in his throat and buried his face in Tobias neck. "You really love me?"

"Yes, sweetheart."

"How can you?" Pete blinked away the threatening tears. "You've only known me for three days." He was having a hard time getting his mind around this. "I know I'm fun in bed, at least I think so, but how can you really love me for that?" He blinked a few more times and then pushed away from Tobias. "If this is some joke, it's not funny."

"It's no joke."

"I think I need some time." Pete got to his feet and went inside. The others quieted as soon as he entered, which likely meant they had been talking about them, which only made him angry. He glared at Elayne and Clarie, and they had the decency to look embarrassed. He wanted someplace to be alone, but there was nowhere. The room he'd been using was now occupied by Lorraine, so he grabbed his phone, turned it on, and groaned when he remembered he had no service.

"The computer is in the office," Tobias said.

Pete nodded, went into the small room, and closed the door behind him. At least he was alone for a few minutes. He turned on the computer, brought up a browser, and logged in to his e-mail.

It was pathetic. Most of what he had were ads for Viagra and credit cards. He deleted them, went to Facebook, and brought up a chat window with Roger.

Are you there?

So you are alive. I was beginning to wonder. How is everything in the wilds?

108

It's nice. Tobias is going to bring me to the meet-up point tomorrow. And then I'll come back. He sent the message and waited for Roger's response, which took a while.

You said he was hot on the phone two days ago. Has anything happened?

Pete groaned, wondering where to begin. There were things he'd never tell Roger. *Yeah.*

Like what? You have to tell me. Is he really as hot as you said? Do you two do the horizontal hula?

Tobias and I were intimate and that's all you get. Horndog!

So are you bringing someone home with you?

Pete sighed. *No. But Tobias is really special and... well, he just told me he loved me, and I freaked out. I mean, how can he love me after three days? Is that possible? Did I say he said he loved ME?* Pete's eyes watered as he typed the last line. *I don't know what to do.*

Why wouldn't he fall in love with you? You're amazing.

I am not. And remember? Me. Shuffled from home to home for years. No one really cared all that damn much. You know that.

So what? We both had shitty luck. That doesn't mean you aren't loveable. I've loved you for years. You're my best friend. Heart. Heart. Heart.

Pete smiled as another message came in.

Don't disbelieve him just because you're scared. If he loves you, truly loves you, then that's something you should carry in your heart.

But I'm leaving. Typing the words helped bring home just what he was going to do.

Love is love. You know that.

How can I leave when he loves me? The lure was so strong just to stay.

Do you love him?

Pete stared at the screen, his fingers poised over the keys. He wasn't sure what to type. *I don't know what love is. I haven't loved anyone in... you know... that way... ever.* He paused and then pressed enter. Pete was truly confused and couldn't believe he was having this kind of conversation over a stupid messenger program.

Okay…? What do you want to do?

I don't know. I have to come home. I have an apartment and a life there. A job. Here, I'm useless. Totally useless. I'm scared of everything….

But……………? Roger could be so dramatic sometimes.

He's really amazing and I may never get to see him again. What if I do love him, and what if he's my one and only chance at happiness? Crap, I'm asking for advice on a stupid messenger. I guess I'm going to have to put on my big-boy pants and do what I have to do. I can't be stupid. Thanks…. He sent what he intended as his last message.

So come home and invite him to come visit you. Maybe you can go visit him again. I don't know.

Me neither. Long-distance things suck, and remember, there's a reason why we're not on the phone. Anyway, I'll call you when I can tomorrow. He sent the message and got a quick okay from Roger, then logged out of the application. Pete wasn't sure what he expected to get from their conversation, but he'd needed to talk to someone. Though he was just as confused as he'd been earlier, his path was a little clearer now. No matter how he felt, he had to go home. The thing was, he and Tobias had had whatever time together they could get and then it was time to return to real life. With his mind made up, he left the office and returned to the living room.

"Where's Tobias?" he asked Clarie, who shrugged. The chill was palpable. "I really need to talk to him."

"I think he's outside."

Pete hurried out, raced around the compound, and found Tobias talking with Katherine. He approached and waited for them to finish their conversation before clearing his throat. "Can I talk to you?"

"I'll let you know once we narrow down his location further." Katherine tilted her head and then turned and walked away.

"I'm sorry for freaking out. It wasn't your fault."

"Okay."

"It's just that no one has told me they loved me…. At least not that I can remember." Pete knew he was probably doing this wrong. "I always figured I wasn't worth loving."

"Why?"

"I think you have to know love in order to understand it. I had foster families. Some of them were very nice. I was with one family for two years and hoped they'd adopt me. Then Mrs. Clark got pregnant and everything changed. They found me another family, and I started all over." Pete tried not to stare down at the ground. "So am I happy that you love me? Yes. And will I remember that you love me once I leave? I don't think I can ever forget it. I mean, I'll always know that no matter what, there was a good man—a strong, decent, kind, caring man—out there somewhere who loves me."

"You don't have to leave. Not if you don't want to."

Pete stood still, a tingling building inside him. "Yes, I do. See, if I stay, you'll realize I belong here about as well as your wolf would be at home in the city. I don't know anything about living out here. You and your pack would be making excuses and carrying my share of the load forever, and I can't have that. They deserve more than that, and so do you." Pete paused and gazed into Tobias's eyes. "I know you all talk about finding your mates, and, well, you deserve to find yours and live happily together."

Tobias pulled him into a hug. "I don't know what to tell you."

"There really isn't anything to say. Tomorrow I'll go home, and the time we had together will be a happy memory for both of us." Pete wanted to cry, but he wasn't going to do that now. There would be plenty of time for loneliness, tears, and God knows what else once he was on the plane and could make it to the bathroom. "We still have the rest of the day together, and maybe if I'm gone, Zev will back off or something. Didn't all this start because you protected me?"

"Maybe. I don't know about that. But if you think you had anything to do with this, you can breathe easy. Zev has been sore ever since he lost the challenge."

"So he didn't like me?"

Tobias shook his head. "I'm sure he did. But is that really important?"

111

"No. I'm sorry. I'm feeling really scatterbrained and more than a little nervous. I like it here, I really do. But I won't be a burden to anyone. I spent too many years being just that, and I won't do that any longer." He'd said what he wanted to, and Pete was prepared for Tobias distancing himself from him. He couldn't blame him. Pete was leaving in the morning, and he—

Tobias kissed him, and whatever had been running through his head pulled to a stop and all his attention settled on Tobias's lips and the strong hands that clasped his ass. "I'm not going to let you go until I have to."

Part of him wished he could stay. Whenever Tobias held him, the worries and cares went away. It was the other times when the doubt crept back in. "Don't you have something you should be doing?"

"Do you want me to leave you alone again?" Tobias loosened his hold.

"No. But I don't want to be the one to keep you from doing what you have to." Pete caught Tobias's gaze. "I see how everyone watches you and looks to you for leadership. You help everyone and always take the time for them. Even Katherine, who is scarier than your sister—and I didn't think that was possible—looks to you for guidance." He was losing his train of thought. "I don't want to get in your way." He also didn't want to spend a minute out of Tobias's sight, and if he could, he'd plaster himself to him. Hell, if he thought he could get Tobias to give him a piggyback ride for the rest of the day, he'd take it.

"Katherine and her folks are out searching for Zev, and we have wolves in the woods patrolling our pack borders. I do need to talk to Fredrick a little more, but for now we are doing what we have to."

"But aren't you supposed to be out there with them instead of here babysitting me?"

"No. I'm staying here where everyone knows where I am and can get in touch with me. I need to protect my mom and sister. That's my role in this at the moment." Tobias patted his back, took his hand, and led Pete inside, where the others were busy chatting.

"Lorraine is doing much better now," Clarie said as she joined them. "She ate fairly well and is resting once again. Sasha is with her, and they're caring for the baby. She'd like to go back to her own cabin."

"Later. I'd like to know where Zev is and what he could be up to before we do that. Katherine, Ryan, and Kaiawa are out there with the others, patrolling and searching for him."

Pete paused, noticing that every set of eyes in the room was on where Tobias held him, Tobias gripped his hand a little tighter. Clarie smiled, and Pete was thankful the earlier cold front was gone.

"Do you want to talk?" Fredrick asked, and Tobias sat in the empty chair and tugged Pete onto his lap. That was dangerous, because being this close to Tobias always got his motor running.

"I'm wondering if there's a way we can use this elemental power Zev has to track him. Can we follow it back?"

Fredrick shook his head. "No. It doesn't act like a tracking system, otherwise they could track me, and that hasn't been the case. I can probably detect if he uses his power and directs it here. Using the power for ill makes the center of whatever is generated black and dark. And there's no way to hide that from me." He leaned closer. "Do you really think he'll try that again? It failed the last time."

"I don't know what he'll try. We could be out here spinning our wheels while Zev has left the area and is laughing at all of us. I think in his heart Zev believes he should be the one to be alpha. I think he always figured that if there was a pack to lead, he'd be the one to do it. So if in his head, deep down, he feels he should be alpha, then that isn't going to go away, and he'll do whatever he thinks he needs to in order to get what he thinks should be rightfully his."

"But your father was alpha here, not his," Clarie said.

"That's true," Pete broke in and turned to Tobias, "but maybe it's bigger than that. You told me that his father was this Anton guy and that he had taken over a lot of packs. So what if he feels he needs to fulfill and rebuild his father's legacy, and he's using this pack as the starting point?"

"That could be it as well," Tobias agreed.

"Granted, both ideas have a similar rationale…."

"But a potentially greater impact and much bigger ramifications. If he's trying to rebuild Anton's empire, then that affects everyone, and that hellish scenario can't happen." Fredrick's expression was nearly as intense as Tobias's.

"So what do we know?" Tobias asked everyone.

"Maybe we should wait until the others get back. They will have valuable insight. Katherine has dealt with my father and brother already, as has Kaiawa. They might be able to help you as well."

The room grew silent for a moment.

"Pete, do you want to help with dinner?" Clarie asked, and Pete turned to Tobias.

"He and I are going to take a short walk. Call if you need either of us—we won't be very far." Tobias's eyes had grown darker, and Pete felt the heat in his gaze.

"We'll be fine here," Clarie said, practically shooing them out the door.

"Okay, what was all that about?" Pete asked as Tobias led him across the compound and into the woods in the direction of the meadow.

"I needed some time alone with you, and if I didn't force it, it wasn't going to happen." They broke into the clearing covered with wildflowers that climbed over what was left of the pack buildings.

"Why here?"

"I've always felt a connection to this place. Yes, pack members died here, but this place isn't sad to me. Being here is a connection to them, a chance to remember what once was and to try to rebuild it." Tobias pulled him close and kissed him hard before Pete could ask his next question, which didn't matter as Tobias's arms enclosed him. "I like coming here to think and try to figure out what I should do."

"What have you decided?" Pete asked. He had no idea what sort of decision was weighing on Tobias, but he was sure he was wrestling with something. "Can I help you with whatever question you're struggling with?"

"I'm afraid not. This is one that I have to figure out on my own." The indecision clouded Tobias's eyes and pinched his features. Pete knew it was important, but he wasn't going to press Tobias. If he wanted him to know, he'd have told him. But Pete wanted to help.

"I could go back to the pack house and leave you alone." He felt like he was intruding, even though Tobias had led him here.

"No." Tobias said quickly but without heat. "I brought you here because I need to think, and you let me do that."

Pete didn't understand any of this, not really, but he settled on a small set of stones that had once been the foundation for one of the dwellings. He closed his eyes and let the sun shine on him. For the first time in weeks, maybe months, his mind was calm and stories began to bubble up. He almost didn't know what to do with them. It had been so long since inspiration struck, but it had now in a very big way.

"What's got you so itchy?"

Pete jumped to his feet. "I need to get a notebook." He raced back toward the pack compound as fast as his legs would take him. He knew the way now and hurried into the house, then down to the guest room. He had to be quiet because Lorraine and the baby were still inside.

She was awake and smiled when he entered.

"I just need to get a notebook." He rummaged in his pack, and once he had what he needed, he took a few seconds to look down at little Edward. Then he left the room and hurried back to the clearing, greeting everyone he passed without slowing down.

"That was fast." Tobias winked at him, and Pete got the idea that Tobias had followed to keep an eye on him.

Pete sat on the ground, his legs folded in front of him, notebook on his lap, and began making notes. He looked up and jotted down how the sky looked here and how the scent of the trees perfuming the air with pine never seemed to go away. It was like nature herself cleaned the outdoors and gave it that heavenly scent.

Tobias stayed where he was, and whenever Pete looked up, Tobias was watching him. They shared a smile, and then Pete went back to work, describing him in detail, from his auburn hair that the sun caught and sometimes transmuted to gold, to his intense eyes that could heat his entire body with just a look. He wanted to remember everything. He even wrote notes about Zev and how he made him feel.

"Are you planning to write about us?"

"No. I won't write about this pack or any details of the people here. That's private, and I would never betray any of your secrets. But there are stories here, and they need to be told." Pete continued writing his notes. Characters came to him, one a lot like Tobias—a leader, strong and sure of himself but unlucky in love and life. He made notes and jotted down the story ideas before they floated away. "It's been a long time since I've had ideas like this."

Tobias remained quiet, and Pete hoped he wasn't mad at him. He'd been working for a while, and when he looked up, Tobias's smile was huge and radiant. He took Pete by the hand. "Are you done for now?"

"Yes. I have enough notes that I'm not going to forget what I was thinking." Pete closed the notebook, and Tobias tugged him to his feet. "Where are we going?"

"To the creek. It's hot, and I thought we could cool off." Tobias led the way through the woods, while Pete took in the tall trees, the scurrying of animals, and the songs of the birds and insects. He wanted to remember everything.

Pete set his notebook on the ground and pulled off his shirt while Tobias stripped down as though it were nothing. Pete had noticed that nudity seemed to not matter to the people here. They took off their clothes to shift and spend time in their wolf forms. It made sense that they didn't think anything of it, but Pete doubted he'd ever become that comfortable with flashing his private bits to everyone. Still, he got his clothes off and waded gingerly into the shrivelingly cold water.

"It's okay. The water is clean."

"It's the cold." Pete shivered. Tobias leaped at him, carried him out, and lowered him into the water.

"Just relax and you'll get used to it."

Pete doubted that, but then he'd do just about anything to be this close to Tobias. Cold water or not, he loved how Tobias felt when they were chest to chest, his hands on Pete's ass, and Pete's cock sliding over Tobias's belly. He could stay like this for hours. "I'm trying, but parts of me are anything but relaxed."

"I know." Tobias lowered him and his cock poked at Pete's ass, teasing him.

"Just don't let me go."

"I'll never do that."

It wasn't Tobias's words that gave him pause, but the way he said it. Pete stilled, letting that sentence roll around in his head. There was something he was missing; he knew it. Tobias's contemplation, the way he'd offered him a place in his pack, the sentimentality from him—all of it added up to something Pete couldn't grasp. He hung on, and Tobias lowered them into the flowing water, letting him float as the creek washed past them.

"You're so beautiful."

"No, I'm not," Pete countered halfheartedly. He wanted to believe, but he'd been told he was nothing special in so many ways, it was hard to believe Tobias when he said differently.

"Yes, you are."

"I'll tell you what's beautiful. Your wolf."

Tobias stood still, the water the only movement around them.

Pete lay on Tobias's hands as it sluiced around him. "He's very beautiful. I remember going to the zoo in Central Park with a school trip, and they had wolves there. I stood at their enclosure, watching them pace back and forth, wondering what they had to be thinking about being penned up."

"I can tell you what they were thinking. Those wolves were wondering what they ever did to deserve to be cooped up and have their freedom taken away. Wolves aren't dogs, and wild wolves will never be pets. We are pack creatures, and we're happiest when we're hunting and running free." Tobias pulled Pete close to him once again. "I hope that's something I never see."

"I never want to again. Not after seeing your pack, and especially you in all your glory. There's something primal and amazing about the way you all run and stay in tune with what's around you." Pete locked gazes with Tobias. "It's sexy."

"We're just who we are."

"No. See, most of the time back home, we try to make nature do what we want. They filled swamps and planted hundreds of trees, even built lakes to make Central Park and have it look natural, but everything is manmade. You'd never do that."

"No. We live with nature. It's part of who we are," Tobias walked him toward the shore and set him on the grass.

"Can I see your wolf?" Pete asked, and Tobias climbed out of the water. Within seconds a huge gray wolf stood where Tobias had been. Pete stroked his head, and Tobias's wolf rubbed against him. "You are handsome, that's for sure." Pete carded his fingers through Tobias's coat, stroking him. Tobias moved closer, pressed Pete back, and straddled him. "Look, I think you're pretty amazing, but don't get any wolfy-sex ideas." Tobias huffed and then sniffed him all over. Pete covered himself and pushed Tobias's nose out of his crotch. "I know you have a thing for smells and all, but like I said, there are limits." Pete hugged Tobias, winding his arms around his neck and resting his head on his back. "You're like a pillow."

Tobias gave him another huff, and Pete closed his eyes, still holding him. It was nice, and Pete loved the feel of Tobias against his skin.

A growl broke Pete's concentration, and Tobias barked and snarled as he moved away, standing between Pete and the cougar that had decided to make an appearance. The cougar pounced, and Tobias leaped, met him, and tore into the cat with his teeth. Blood sprayed as Pete tried to get out of the way.

The cat skidded as it landed and got back to its feet. It was moving more slowly now, and Tobias stayed between him and it. The cat hissed, not giving up, and Pete tensed as it pounced once again. Tobias was ready, his teeth cutting deep. The cougar didn't get up again, and Tobias raised his head, howling to the sky, blood on his muzzle.

Pete hurried to where he'd set his clothes, wanting to put them on. Before he could, Tobias loped over, and Pete hugged him, stroking his back. "You protected me."

Tobias pressed closer, and Pete wished he could talk in this form, but Tobias's eyes said plenty. Then, within seconds, a naked and very human Tobias stood over him. "Of course I protected you. You're my—" Tobias cut himself off and hurried into the stream. He submerged and popped out of the water, rubbing his chest and face. "You should get back in here and clean up."

Pete remembered the blood and got in the water as some of the others burst out of the forest. Pete hated being naked in front of a crowd, and while this one was small, he wanted to sink under the water and disappear.

Tobias pulled him lower so they were both in the water and mostly out of prying eyes. "We're fine," he told Sasha, who stood nearest the body of the cougar. "Find a place to bury her so we can give her back to the Mother."

"Very well." Sasha lifted the body and carried it away, leading the others along with him.

"We won't be too long."

"Katherine and the others are back. I'll tell them you'll be up soon." They stepped into the woods, and once again Pete and Tobias were alone.

"That should freak me out."

"What?"

"Being followed and attacked by that same cougar. But it doesn't. You'll protect me from anything."

"Always. As long as you're with me, you're mine to protect." Tobias kissed him hard as he rose out of the water. "It's part of being the pack alpha."

"Is that the only reason?" Pete asked.

"You know it isn't." Tobias kissed him again, and this time he didn't stop, taking possession of Pete's mouth until his lips tingled and then grew almost numb. Pete poured all the deep feelings built inside him, the ones he hadn't dared speak about, into the kiss. If he gave them voice, then he was scared he'd never be able to contain them.

"I do know." Pete stroked Tobias's forehead and then brought their lips together once more. The water slipped from his body as Tobias climbed out of the creek and laid him on the soft grass.

"I need you." Tobias's gravelly voice was more than Pete could take. He clung to Tobias, legs fastened around his waist. He was ready and waiting, and Pete expected Tobias to enter him. He'd already closed his eyes, preparing to be breached dry, but nothing happened.

He slid his eyes open, and Tobias got to his knees, hefted Pete over his shoulder, and carried him bareass naked though the woods toward the compound.

"Tobias!" Pete struggled halfheartedly, trying to stomp down his rising embarrassment and consternation, until he realized he had amazing access to Tobias's backside. He stretched his hands and glommed onto Tobias's hard buttcheeks, unashamedly feeling him up. "If you can show my ass to everyone, then I can grab yours."

Tobias walked faster, and the sun broke on them when they left the shade of the trees. No one said anything—not that Pete paid attention to anything other than Tobias's ass and a few legs and feet.

"Tobias!" Clarie snapped, and Tobias actually growled at his mother.

Pete smacked his butt for that, momentarily forgetting that his own butt was on prominent display to Tobias's mother. He was going to die of embarrassment at any moment.

Tobias only slowed to open the door to his room and then flipped Pete on the bed. "You're going tomorrow…."

As though that explained everything.

Tobias looked him over from head to toe, even sniffing him before climbing on the bed. Tobias's eyes were feral and dark. There was none of the usual licking and touching. Tobias held him tightly, pressing to him, and when Pete opened himself to him, Tobias reached for lube by the side of the bed. After the fastest preparation in history, Tobias slid into him in a long, slow movement. "My wolf needs to know that you're okay and that you're his." Tobias filled him deep, and Pete gasped and clenched around him. "That cougar tried to take you."

"She was hungry."

"No. She was asserting her dominance." Tobias snapped his hips. "And I will not have that as far as you're concerned. You're here, you're my guest, and you're—" Tobias bit his lower lip hard enough that Pete was afraid Tobias was going to draw blood. He'd never thought possessiveness could be hot, but this sure as hell was. "No one hurts someone I love if I can help it."

Pete got the impression Tobias had originally intended to say more, but he forgot all about it when Tobias pulled him into a kiss and continued snapping his hips. Soft growls emanated from Tobias's throat, and the intensity in his eyes didn't diminish. "I feel like I'm making love to both of you."

Tobias swallowed. "You are." He moved faster, hitting Pete in just the right place, making him fly over and over again, pushing him higher.

"Tell me about it later." Pete wound his arms around Tobias's neck, watching as his eyes visibly changed to deep amber. Tobias shook, and when Pete kissed him, Tobias nibbled on his lips.

Everything was more intense than ever before. Pete was fuller, each touch was more meaningful, with the added energy that Tobias exuded from every pore. It truly was as though something inside him was trying to get out. Pete wasn't sure how to keep the electricity between them from taking over. His eyes crossed and he was hyperaware of everything to do with Tobias.

"Jesus!" Pete held tighter as Tobias moved quicker.

"I know." Tobias buried his face in Pete's neck and licked and sucked hard. Pete was going to have one heck of a mark, but he didn't care in the least. He was too far gone, his mind taken over by the intensity of the passion between them.

Pete wasn't usually a silent guy in bed. He liked sexy talk, but there was no need for it this time. He knew what Tobias wanted, and it was as if Tobias was reading his mind. If he needed more, Tobias gave it to him, and when he came close to the edge, Tobias pulled back until he felt like he was about to shatter into a million pieces. Then, when Pete was to the point where he couldn't hold it together any longer, Tobias stroked his cock hard and fast until Pete saw stars as he tumbled over the edge, with Tobias following right behind.

Pete floated for a long time and came back to himself when Tobias gently withdrew and then licked up his belly. He shivered and cradled Tobias's head, stroking his fingers through his hair. "How much do you want to bet that we scared away the rest of the pack?"

"That's likely." Tobias closed his eyes and rested his head on Pete's shoulder.

"Is your wolf happy?"

"Yes. You are all we need." Tobias kissed him and hugged him close, rubbing his chest against Pete's back.

"Are you marking me?"

"Kind of." Tobias chuckled but didn't stop. "I want you to smell like me long after you go home." He stilled and then groaned. "I have to get up and see what's going on." He rolled Pete onto his back. "Stay here if you're tired, but Katherine is going to need me."

"You have responsibilities."

Tobias got up and put on some clothes. He also laid out some for Pete and left the room.

Grateful he wasn't going to have to go naked to get his own clothes from the room Lorraine was using, Pete pulled on the clothes. They were too big for him, but the sweatpants and dark blue T-shirt smelled like Tobias and that was enough. He didn't care how they fit. He'd also borrowed a pair of Tobias's shoes. They were a little big as well, but it was better than going barefoot, since the clothes he'd been wearing were probably still at the creek.

The house was indeed empty, and it seemed Lorraine had left the room with little Edward. Pete saw Tobias outside and wondered if he should join him. He exited the house and went over to where Tobias was holding his confab.

"He's holed up in a trailer outside of town," Greg said excitedly. "He was doing his best to hide his scent."

"How?" Katherine asked.

"Bounce dryer sheets and Downy. That's why it took us so long to find him. That stuff is so strong that...." Greg sneezed and shook his head. "I still can't get it out of my nose. He had those dang sheets everywhere, I swear. We kept losing him, and then Kaiawa caught his scent."

"Actually, it was Stephan," Kaiawa corrected with a gentle smile that struck Pete as telling. Kaiawa seemed like the quiet, stoic type.

Fredrick nudged Pete slightly and tilted his head in Stephan and Kaiawa's direction, winking.

"That's good work," Katherine said. "But what are we going to do about it?"

"Do you think he caught your scents?" Pete asked. "If he was going to great lengths to hide his, it might interfere with his ability to smell you, but I suspect he's also on heightened alert too."

They exchanged looks with one another. "No. I think if he had, he'd have bugged out quickly. Stephan and I stayed behind for a while to watch him, and he stayed put. Now that we know what to smell for, we should be able to find him pretty easily, even if he has moved."

"Very good." Tobias grinned at him. "I think we need to watch him. See what he's doing and where he goes." He turned to Katherine. "Can we use one of your people? He isn't as likely to spook if he catches their scent."

"Christopher and I can go," Fredrick offered. "There was a store and bar there. Even if he sees or scents us, we can act like patrons."

"Good idea. But before you leave, I suggest you bathe and make sure you take nothing with you that smells of this pack." Katherine

123

tossed Christopher the keys to the truck. "Report back to us this evening, and be sure to let us know if you think he's going to make a move. There's no phone service here, so message us."

"I can monitor the e-mail," Pete offered, wanting to be part of this somehow.

Tobias gave them the e-mail address, and they got ready to go. He addressed the rest of the group. "I have a feeling it's going to be a long night, so the rest of us should lie low and try to sleep if we can. You've all been going for hours. I'll keep watch, and we'll meet after dark once Christopher and Fredrick return." They filed away, and Tobias turned to him. "I need to mark the perimeter."

That was something Pete didn't need to see. "I'll help Clarie with dinner and check on Lorraine." Pete leaned in for a kiss and then went to Lorraine and Sasha's cabin.

Sasha said Edward was feeding when he knocked on the door, so Pete explained that he'd bring dinner over for them when it was ready and then went into the kitchen to get started.

PETE COULD not believe how tired he was. It seemed as though he'd packed a week of activity into a single day. He and Clarie made dinner, he brought some to Sasha and Lorraine, and then he went to lie down. He fell asleep as soon as his head hit the pillow.

When he woke, the house was quiet, and no light came through his window. He yawned, got up, and padded through the house trying to find Tobias. No one seemed to be around, and even the compound was free of voices and conversation. He wondered if he should call for Tobias, but didn't want to disturb him if he was in a strategy session.

Pete thought to try the other side of the house to see if Christopher and Fredrick were back. He opened the door and stepped outside, not seeing much beyond the shaft of light that spilled out the door. He stepped beyond that light and a hand clamped over his mouth. Pete struggled, but his legs felt weak and then everything went black.

CHAPTER 8

SOMETHING WAS wrong. Tobias knew it the same way he knew the weather was going to change or one of his pack members was hurting. His gut ached, and he had no idea why. They had their plan of attack and everything was falling into place. He shouldn't feel this way, and yet the unsettledness inside wouldn't go away.

"What do you think is wrong with the plan?" Ryan asked as they walked back to the pack house from where they'd been meeting in Brick and Greg's cabin.

"Nothing."

"Then why do you look like you just ate bad meat?"

"Something is coming. I...." As he got closer to the house, Tobias inhaled, slowed his strides as he scented the air again, and picked up his pace. "Zev has been here."

"What?" Ryan followed right behind him as Tobias burst into the pack house, and scented everything. But the inside was clear. The scent was outside, and when he opened the other door, it came through loud and clear. So did the chemical smell that hung in the air. He nearly gagged on it, and his wolf growled and paced inside him.

"Zev has Pete." He could smell both of them together.

"Yeah. And he drugged him. Not sure what it is."

"Get everyone together, now!"

Ryan took off, and Tobias forced air into his lungs and made his mind work. He had to stay calm so he could figure out a plan of attack. Running off, the way every instinct told him to, was not going to get Pete back, even though his gut felt like it had been ripped in two.

"What happened?" Brick said, grinding to a stop in front of Tobias.

"Zev has Pete."

Katherine scented the air and nodded her agreement. "It sure smells that way."

"Greg and Brick, can you track them?" Tobias asked.

"Yes."

"Then let's go. Christopher and Fredrick, go with Greg and Brick. Since you saw Zev at the bar and he didn't react to you, you need to get back there and let us know if he's there. We'll follow behind you and stay out of sight until you call. There is cell service in town, but we need to be careful. Zev is going to be on high alert, and I suspect he wants me to come after him." Which was exactly what Tobias's wolf screamed at him to do. His mate was in trouble, and his wolf would do anything to get him back.

"We're on it," Brick said, glancing cautiously at Greg, who took a single step back and looked down. Tobias could feel the discomfort between them, but it was a testament to both of them that they hurried to the truck together and pulled out of the compound.

Everyone else moved en masse toward the other truck.

"We can't all go," Tobias said.

"But we want to help Pete," Hayden told him.

"Then Sasha and Ryan will stay here to protect the compound—and Lorraine and Edward—and the rest of us will go." He wasn't sure what they were going to do once they got there. They would have to see the lay of the land. Meanwhile, Pete was in danger, and there was no way Tobias could get that out of his head.

He did know one thing for sure: if Zev hurt Pete, there would be total fucking hell to pay.

TOBIAS'S WOLF paced in his mind as he crouched in the trees, in wolf form, watching the small rental trailer. The scent of dryer sheets made him want to sneeze every few minutes, but he held it in, even when the breeze blew it toward him in full force. At least that crap would help hide his scent from Zev.

Anger seethed inside him, and when the air stilled, he could catch faint whispers of Pete's voice. It was barely a squeak, but it pinged his wolf hearing like a foghorn. There was no doubt Pete was in there, and it didn't take much for Tobias to understand the fear he was feeling. It was rolling off Pete, ebbing and flowing like a wave on the sand.

Greg approached him from behind in wolf form, with Brick nearby.

What do you know? he sent to both of them. Unfortunately they wouldn't be able to communicate back.

Greg signaled, and Tobias moved deeper into cover and then shifted. Greg did the same.

"Pete is in there. I was able to get close enough to smell him. He's really scared, but I didn't smell blood. I think I'm getting pretty good at discounting the scents Zev's using to hide."

"What do you think?"

"If we attack, he'll hurt Pete first thing. Zev is jittery, and who knows what's going on with him. I wish I knew more. We've got to lure him outside. It's the only way."

Tobias nodded and thought for a few minutes.

"We could call the sheriff," Greg offered as Katherine and the others approached and shifted. They went still deeper into the trees, leaving Brick to keep watch.

"I say we surround the place, then lure him out. We can get around the building and call to each other. He'll hear it and know he's surrounded," Katherine said.

"What if he hurts Pete?" Tobias nearly growled. This was too damn frightening for words. Letting his mate go was one thing—at least he'd know he was out there—but if anything happened to him, Tobias would grieve for the rest of his life.

Katherine visibly backed down and some of her confidence slipped from her eyes. That was a good thing as far as Tobias was concerned. It meant she was starting to think through options other than the full-on attack.

"What do you think Zev really wants?" she asked. "I mean, you've said he wants the pack, but I doubt any of the wolves here would follow him. The pack would disintegrate if he were to become the alpha. Everyone has been through too much crap to go through all that again, and Zev has to know that on some level. So what does he really want?"

It took Tobias a second to answer the question. "Me." He knew that was true. "Zev made a play for Pete when they first met, and I spoiled whatever game he was playing."

"And now Pete has your scent on him, and Zev is going to know the two of you have been intimate, so he took what he thinks belongs to you." Katherine nodded as she thought. "We could give him what he wants."

The others began talking at the same time, and Tobias hushed them all, thankful they were a distance away from the cabin. "Half the forest will hear you," he chastised to quell their excitement. "Maybe that's the answer."

"No," Greg protested, voice quiet and filled with fear. "We can't lose you."

"You won't. Not if we do this right. I'll approach the cabin, and the rest of you are going to stay close and out of sight. You have to stay downwind so he doesn't catch your scent. I have no intention of going inside, but I will if I think I can help Pete." He looked at each pack member in turn. "I know all of you have my back, but I have to get Pete out of there." The thought of what Zev might have done to Pete already was enough to make his blood boil.

"All right," Hayden agreed as the others nodded their assent.

"Katherine is in charge." He locked gazes with the strong wolf. Part of him rebelled at allowing another wolf to take control of his pack members, but she had more than proven herself to be a good friend and someone he could rely on. "She'll know when to act."

"Spread out and get into position."

"How will we know when to move in?" Greg asked.

Katherine called like a hawk, a near exact imitation.

"Go on. I want you in position before I approach the cabin." Tobias waited while they all quietly melted into the woods. He gave them enough time to get into place and then walked back to the road and approached the cabin that way.

"Zev," Tobias called from fifty feet away. The area around was deserted, with only a dim light coming from inside the cabin. The scents Zev had used to try to cover his own had dissipated a bit, and Tobias could smell Pete's fear and the acidic scent of pain. Zev had hurt him somehow. Tobias wished he could see inside that cabin. "Zev, come out here."

Tobias stopped walking. He knew Zev could hear him, but the cabin remained quiet, with no movement. "I'm waiting." He used his best authoritative alpha voice, knowing that would get to Zev, and within a few seconds, the door opened. A dim crest of light shone onto the wood-chip path in front of it. Tobias could see partially inside, but Pete wasn't visible.

"Toby... I was wondering when you'd show up for your little toy."

Tobias seethed. "Let him go. You know nothing good will come from any of this. He has nothing to do with what's between the two of us."

Zev took a step outside the door, smiling a knowing grin that set Tobias's teeth on edge. "Why? You didn't want him." Zev took one more step and then stopped and turned to look back inside.

"This is kidnapping, and you know that isn't the way we do things. Start acting like a wolf and have some dignity and self-respect. Let Pete go, and I'll let you turn around and leave. You know you don't belong here." Tobias took a few steps closer and to the side, hoping for a better view of the cabin interior.

Zev moved back, blocking the doorway. "I know what you're doing." He quickly glanced inside. "I haven't hurt him yet. But I can certainly understand what you see in him. He is a pretty little thing."

"You had better not touch him! Ever!" Tobias growled, and then wished he hadn't let Zev bait him like that. The purpose of this was to get Zev on edge. Tobias took a deep breath and calmed himself. Zev would be able to read him and would know he was getting bothered.

Zev faced him again. "What do you care? He's just a human and doesn't mean anything to us."

Tobias heard Pete's muffled cry and knew Pete was gagged. He'd suspected it, but knowing it made him angry. "Everyone is important."

"Bullshit. This human means something to you. Your scent was all over him." Zev turned back inside and then out toward him. "I know you have a plan, but I don't intend to go along with any of it. You have wolves out there, most likely downwind. But I'm not coming out, and you're not coming in."

Tobias moved closer, and he could feel Zev's gaze drilling into him. Zev actually took a few steps forward and leaned in a little. Tobias stilled and schooled his expression—or at least, he tried to. "Zev, just let him go."

Zev glanced inside, and when he turned back to Tobias, the evil joy in Zev's eyes made his stomach turn to ice. "Have you even told him that he's your mate?" Zev's lips curved into a smile. "You haven't, have you? This man you're so desperate to rescue doesn't even know the reason why. That he's the other half of your soul." Zev chuckled like some villain in a second-rate movie, and Tobias clenched his fists. "That's absolutely beautiful. Your mate is a human, and I heard he's supposed to leave tomorrow. How does that work? I know you haven't bonded with him or else...."

"That's enough!" Tobias roared as his anger threatened to get the better of him.

"No, it's not. It's perfect. I have your mate. I knew the human meant something to you, but I had no idea he was the other half of your world. Now I need to see just how much I can use that to make you pay."

Tobias moved still closer.

"Stop or I'll go inside and gut him like a fish. You'll be able to smell your mate's blood as it wets the floorboards of the trailer. Now that's justice."

"How is kidnapping justice?" Tobias pressed. "You know our way of life. Mom did her best to teach it to you."

"Bullshit. I learned how things are from my father and his family. I know the truth. In this life, you have to take what you want because no one is going to give it to you. And right now I intend to take everything I possible can from you." His eyes darkened. "I'm going to take it all, your mate and your pack."

"How do you plan to do that?" Tobias asked, surprisingly calm now that his surge of anger had dissipated. He needed to keep his head as he looked for a way to get Pete out of this situation.

The crash of broken glass sounded from inside the trailer, and Zev hurried inside and slammed the door closed.

"Tobias!" Pete cried over the sound of more glass breaking.

Tobias raced forward and heard the call go up from inside the woods. The others were on their way, but he wasn't going to stop. Pete was in immediate danger. Tobias reached the door, shifted his legs, and kicked it in. The door splintered, and Tobias stood tall, huffing, looking at Zev as he held Pete down. Blood was spattered over the floor, and it took him only a second to scent that it was from both Pete and Zev.

Pete struggled and managed to kick Zev in the balls.

Zev inhaled sharply. "I'll kill you for that." He reached back, but Tobias grabbed his hand and ripped it back until bone snapped.

Zev howled in pain, but Tobias didn't stop. He used the momentum to pull Zev away and toss him aside so he could get to Pete, who lay in blood with shards of broken glass everywhere. Pieces dug into Tobias's feet, but he leaned down to cradle Pete into his arms as the others arrived. Tobias looked up in time to see Zev shift and then leap out the window Pete must have broken, leaving behind blood and hair on the jagged edges of the glass.

Katherine sprang out of the cabin. Tobias gently lifted Pete off the floor and put him on the bed in the corner.

"What should we do?" Greg asked after shifting.

Tobias turned to him. "Get everyone around the cabin to keep us safe and make sure Zev doesn't try to come back." Tobias shifted again to fully human and turned back to Pete. "Where are you cut?" His heart still raced, the scent of Pete's blood still strong in his nose. He wanted to go after Zev and rip him to pieces, but he was needed right here by his mate. Pete was more important.

131

"On my leg." Pete gritted his teeth as Tobias ripped his pant leg to expose a gash with a shard of glass still inside.

"Is that all?"

"Yeah. The rest of the blood was Zev's. I got him good with a pitcher once I could get my hands free."

"Hold still." Tobias hurried to the bathroom and found what looked like a clean cloth, grabbed it, and then returned to Pete. He tugged the glass out of Pete's leg as gently as he could and covered the wound with the cloth, applying pressure to stop the bleeding.

"God, that's better." Pete sighed and lay back on the bed.

"How did you get loose?"

"That guy is a real asshole, but he doesn't know shit about knots, so I was able to work my hands loose. I thought that if I could break a window, I could get out, or at least cause enough of a diversion that you could get him."

"The diversion part worked, but you weren't supposed to get hurt."

"Believe me, that wasn't part of the plan." Pete hissed as Tobias lifted the cloth and saw the bleeding had slowed. The cut didn't seem to be too deep, which was a relief. Tobias wrapped Pete's leg with the dry cloth, then bound it with a strip torn from his now-ruined pants. "So how did Zev get hurt? There's a lot of blood on the floor."

"I broke a vase over his back. I know he was cut pretty bad, but he came at me anyway, and then you got here." Pete hugged him tightly, shaking, and Tobias let go of the questions and returned the hug. He inhaled, ignoring the lingering scent of blood and concentrating on the deeper scent of his mate.

"What did Zev mean about me being your mate?" Pete didn't let go. "Is it true?"

"Yes." There was no way he could lie about that.

Pete let go. "Why didn't you tell me?"

Tobias sighed and thought for a second to try to put together an accurate answer.

"Zev is gone," Katherine said as she came inside, now dressed. Her clothes were disheveled, and Tobias knew she'd simply yanked them on. "I followed his trail as long as I dared and then thought it best to return to make sure everyone was okay. I believe he shifted and then shifted back to wolf form because the blood trail stopped abruptly."

Tobias wanted to scream. He had hoped he could get Pete away and take out Zev once and for all, but that wasn't happening. "Was he heading toward the compound?"

Katherine shook her head. "He was running for the hills like the coward he is. No self-respecting wolf would ever take someone like that. They'd challenge you straight on if they had any courage at all."

Tobias was growing to like Katherine more and more. "I agree. Let's make sure everyone is dressed and get them into the trucks. We need to get back to the compound as quickly as we can."

"What about the mess in the trailer?"

"Zev made it. Let him fix it. He rented the place somehow, so he can deal with the mess he made. Just clean up any signs of any of us and let's get out of here. More than anything, make sure it looks like a natural wolf got inside and might have hurt someone."

She nodded, and Tobias lifted Pete into his arms, carried him out to his truck, and laid him carefully in the passenger seat. The others joined them pretty quickly, piling into the other truck, which had a backseat, and then they all took off toward the compound, Katherine leading and Tobias following.

Keep to the speed limit and don't draw any attention, he sent telepathically to Katherine, who immediately slowed down.

"I'm okay. You don't need to keep looking at me like I'm going to die at any moment. Just keep your eyes on the road."

Tobias gripped the wheel tighter and did as Pete asked.

Pete sighed loudly, and Tobias knew what was coming. "Were you ever going to tell me that I was your mate?" The edge to Pete's voice hurt, even though he expected it.

"Honestly? No."

"Why not? Are you ashamed that I'm your mate?"

Tobias pressed the brake and let the other truck speed away. He pulled the truck to the side of the road and threw it into park. "No.

Never. I didn't tell you because it doesn't matter. I already know the man that you are, and if I told you that you were my mate…." There was no use going on. This whole conversation wasn't going to change anything. "Tomorrow you need to go home. That's where your life is. Not here." He put the truck in gear and built a brick wall around his heart to keep it from shattering into little pieces. "There will always be a part of you that stays with me. I can guarantee that, and I will never forget you. But your life is back in New York. You said so yourself. It isn't here, and I can't live there."

"But you only get one mate?"

"How do you know that?"

"What do you think your mother and I do when we cook, stand around and say nothing? We yammer like fools, and she told me about how mates work. She said that you only get one."

"Yes. That's true, and you will always be my mate no matter where you are." He blinked to keep the heartbreak off his expression. "But you can't stay, and if I told you, then you would."

"Of course I would, you asshole!" Pete shouted.

"Then that's why I didn't. You'd give up your life to make me happy, but you deserve to be happy as well. So forget all about this mate stuff. I'm not going anywhere, and I will be fine knowing you're out there living a happy life. That's all I want for you." Tobias grew quiet and sped up, driving through the tunnel of trees that his headlights illuminated. "You know I'm right."

When Pete didn't argue, Tobias relaxed a little. He knew in his heart that he was doing the right thing, even if he was going to pay a heavy price for it. Pete had made his choice.

Tobias was grateful as they rode in silence. At least it gave him a chance to think and not talk. Nevertheless, the tension between them built with each passing mile and each bump that shook the vehicle. More than once Pete groaned, and Tobias knew he was aching. He was also well aware that his psychotic half brother was responsible, which only added to his own guilt.

Finally he made the turn off the rocky lane and onto the drive near the pack house. Tobias wanted to open the door, race to the woods, shift, and run until he fell down. But his mate needed to get inside, and he had other responsibilities, so what he wanted was third on the list of things he could do at the moment. Instead he got out, walked around to Pete's door, opened it, and offered to help him.

"I'm perfectly capable of making it inside on my own." Pete hobbled to the ground and then gingerly limped toward the door. "Are you coming or are you just going to stand there?" The anger rolled off Pete, and damn it all if Tobias could do nothing but follow him. He knew he'd hurt his mate and he wanted to try to make it better, but there was no way he could think of to do that.

Once inside, Pete continued through the house and down to his room without looking back.

"What happened?" Tobias's mother asked gently.

"Zev... he figured out that Pete was my mate and let the cat out of the bag, and now Pete thinks I'm ashamed of him."

He expected support and sympathy from his mother. What he got was a smack on the side of the head that completely stunned him.

"What was that for?"

"I've been quiet up until now because I hoped you'd pull your head out of your butt." She huffed and stepped closer. "You're the leader, the alpha, and you take good care of all of us. You always put everyone ahead of yourself. That's what makes you a good leader, but what will make you a great one is being happy." She pointed toward the hall. "He can make you happy."

"Yes, probably. But he has a life, and it isn't here. I don't want him to stay just because he's my mate and the only one I'm ever going to get. That isn't fair to him."

"Maybe not. But you never asked him. You simply assumed the answer and went on. You're used to making decisions, but you can't always make all of the decisions for everyone else. This is one you probably should have told him about and then let him decide. It isn't just your life we're talking about, but his as well."

Tobias groaned. He hated when his mother was right. "Okay. But was hitting necessary?"

"Sometimes you can be as stubborn as a mule, and that's a surefire attention-getter. Now go on and talk to him." She turned and went back into the kitchen, where she began making food for everyone. If there was excitement that needed to be smoothed out, or comfort to be given, his mother was sure to be in the kitchen. "Come get something to eat in a little while."

Tobias knew his mother was correct, but he went outside and made sure everyone in the pack was all right first. Then he checked on Lorraine and the pup, who were both asleep, before returning to the pack house. Everyone was where they should be. With more trepidation than if he were approaching a challenge, he went into the bedroom, where he found Pete sitting on the edge of the bed.

"How is your leg?"

Pete lifted his gaze, eyes thunderous. "So you were just going to let me go without saying a single word about me being your mate." He slowly got to his feet, seeming a little wobbly, but that didn't change his expression for a second. "You know, your mother's right. You're as stubborn as a mule, and if I could, I'd kick your ass from here to New York. You knew I was your mate the entire time I was here, didn't you?"

"Yes. You have the most amazing smell. Best in the world. I could pick you out of a crowd of a million people just by closing my eyes and following my nose." Tobias looked down and Pete followed his gaze to the bulge in his pants. "Just being next to you does that to me. I was uncomfortable the entire ride in the car because if I smell you, see you, or just hear your voice, I want you more than anything."

"Then why didn't you say something? You know all you had to do was be honest." Pete rolled his eyes. "How many people are going to wake up after sleeping in your storage shed and just accept that you are what you are? Did I cause trouble? No. Did I try to help and fit in?" Pete put his hands on his hips. "See, I'm not the one who has trouble accepting who they are. That's you."

"How do you figure that?"

Pete glared at him. "I was willing to accept that you're a shifter and part wolf. I also am willing to tell no one that people like you exist. Think about that. No one out there knows about you, and I can't tell them because if I do, you'll all be in danger. So I'll keep my mouth shut about the most amazing group of people I've ever met and just go home." He limped forward a little more. "See, this wonderful group of people had a leader who is so dense and such a… dickweed… that he meets his mate"—Pete waved his hands in the air—"the one person destined for him, and he's such a stubborn ass who thinks he knows everything that he doesn't tell him and wants him to leave." He pulled open the bedroom door. "Well, you're going to get your wish. Tomorrow I'm going back to town to meet the party from the ridiculous tour group that fucking left me behind, and I'm going home. Now you're leaving so I can take all of three minutes to pack."

Tobias stood gaping. It was all he could do. His mouth hung open, and he moved toward the door. Once he was out of the room, he turned back to Pete, only to have the door slammed in his face.

He knew he'd messed up, but as hard as this was, he was getting what he wanted.

Tobias returned to the kitchen and sat at one of the stools while his mother got something together for a late-evening snack.

The rest of the pack wandered in, except Sasha and Lorraine. His mother asked Greg to take some food over to them, and when he returned, everyone squeezed in around the table, talking over and rehashing the evenings events.

Tobias heard the door open at the end of the hallway and turned when Pete entered the room. The conversation immediately stopped as tension grew. Greg and Brick looked at each other in some sort of silent communication, took their plates, and went outside. Katherine, Christopher, Fredrick, Stephan, and Kaiawa all did the same thing. Even Clarie followed them outside.

Pete went to the counter, got a plate, and took a single sandwich. Then he turned, and Tobias got his first look at the tear tracks running down his cheeks.

"Sweetheart."

"Tobias, there's nothing you can say. I'm angry you didn't tell me the truth, but you're right. It doesn't change things. I have to go home and go back to my real life. But this has been the best time I've ever had, and who thought getting lost would…." Pete set his plate down on the table and turned away. Tobias jumped to his feet, pulling Pete into a hug that his body reacted to with incredible gusto. "Look, I know…. I need to get my leg cleaned up and bandaged." Pete pulled away and hurried back to his room.

Tobias was torn, wondering if he should follow Pete, but his reaction had made his feelings very clear, and Tobias left the pack house and joined the others outside.

They sat in a circle. Stephan sat next to Kaiawa, leaning against him, the two of them whispering, while everyone else did their best to politely ignore them and give them some privacy.

"It's about time those two got together," Katherine whispered to him. "I've watched them circle each other for so long…."

Kaiawa stood and took Stephan's hand, leading him toward the woods. After a few minutes, a howl, followed by a second, went up and wound between the trees. The joy in both of them was clear as a bell.

Christopher and Fredrick were the next to leave, and as the others finished eating, they left as well, leaving Tobias alone with Katherine and his mother.

"I think Zev is long gone by now." Katherine stood after her pronouncement. "I'm going to take my guys, and we'll leave tomorrow. It'll take a week or more for him to recover from the injuries I saw."

"Of course," Tobias agreed. He couldn't keep Mikael's people here forever. They had families to return to.

"If you get wind of him, just call and we'll have your back." They shook hands, and then she left and it was just Tobias and his mother, who crossed her arms over her chest, glaring at him.

"You can't leave things like this with your mate."

"What do you want me to do? He's going to leave regardless."

"Yes. That's true. But he's your mate." His mother let her arms fall and blinked her eyes. "You only get one mate, and I can't believe you aren't willing to fight for him. You'd fight for any of us, but not for him." She sniffed.

"This isn't about fighting, Mom. It's about loving him enough to let him have his own life and be happy. I always knew love required sacrifice, but I didn't realize it would cost me my heart and a part of my soul." Tobias stood and walked back toward the pack house. His mother was right about one thing: he didn't want things to stay this way between them.

Tobias went inside and down to Pete's room. The door was still closed. He almost turned to go to his own room. "Screw it." He twisted the knob, went inside, and silently closed the door.

Pete lay on his side with his back to him and didn't move. Tobias might have wondered if he was asleep, but his wolf senses told him Pete was playing possum. After the last few hours, Tobias didn't blame him, and he probably should have left him alone, but that was impossible. He had to be here with him. Tobias was drawn to Pete like a wolf was drawn to howl at the moon.

Tobias sat on the edge of the bed, and Pete slowly rolled over. "I'm sorry I hurt you." Words seemed inadequate for what he was feeling. In a way, Tobias knew he'd messed up, but if he took the time to really think, it was doubtful he'd change anything.

"I know you did it because you were trying to protect me." Pete slowly sat up. "But I don't need your protection, not from this and not from you." He rubbed his eyes. "What time is it?"

"Late. Most everyone has gone to bed." Tobias hoped Pete took the hint. He didn't want to go back to his own bed tonight. Pete seemed to have the same idea. He shifted back to give Tobias more room, and Tobias leaned over him and took Pete's lips in a deep kiss. The bed creaked slightly as he moved.

Pete moaned softly, and Tobias took his time. This was very likely the last time he'd be with his mate like this, and Tobias needed to make the most of it. He had every intention of seeing Pete writhe and moan under him as he made those amazing sounds that Tobias would commit to memory so he could replay them on the lonely nights he was sure lay ahead.

Tobias slowly removed Pete's clothes, kissing and touching every inch of him to memorize the little things, like the divot above his hip bone and the way his stomach fluttered when Tobias licked around his belly button. All of it he held deep down inside so he'd never forget any of Pete.

Minutes stretched to hours as Tobias loved Pete, making sure he communicated everything he felt deep in his heart. This was his one and only chance, and Tobias was determined to make it good. When he entered Pete, their gazes locked. Pete's eyes blazed with heat and the passion that seared itself deep into Tobias brain. As he moved, Pete moved with him, gasping, moaning, whimpering his own cadences of love. Tobias knew Pete loved him, and that both heated his desire and added to his worry.

Pete held him tightly when the passion built and threatened to overwhelm both of them. This was what he wanted, and Tobias buried his face against Pete's neck. His teeth elongated, every instinct and desire telling him to strike and make Pete his forever. If Tobias mated him, Pete wouldn't be able to stay away from him. He'd need Tobias just as much as Tobias needed him. His gums ached and his wolf urged him forward to claim their mate and take what they both wanted.

Tobias's brain clouded as instinct rose higher and higher, beat a fever pitch at the base of his brain, sent a rush of endorphins coursing through him, urged Tobias to do what nature intended. For a few seconds, Tobias nearly gave in, even wondered if that was what the Mother wanted him to do. As Tobias's desire reached a near-peak and Pete groaned loudly, bucking up against him, Tobias nearly lost it, even scraped his teeth over the tender, luscious skin of Pete's neck.

When Pete's climax broke over him, he yelled at the top of his lungs, the cry echoing through Tobias's head. It drove him higher, his release nearly on him. Tobias pulled his head away, thrust forward with everything he had, turned his head toward the roof, and howled his release, frustration, and pent-up desire through the ceiling and roof and up to the star-filled sky he knew hung above them all. Tobias had made his decision, and he wouldn't take Pete's choice away from him no matter what, even if his own heart shattered in the process.

Wrung out and covered in sweat, Tobias heaved air into his lungs and howled once again, softer this time and more plaintively. Then he leaned down and kissed Pete with everything he had. The rush of lovemaking slowly ebbed away once their bodies separated, and Tobias lay next to Pete, holding him in the sweet haze of momentary happiness.

"Tobias…," Pete whispered.

"Hmmmm." Tobias listened in the darkness, keeping his eyes closed. "I know you need to be at the meeting place at noon, and I'll have you there in time. Just close your eyes and go to sleep." He held Pete closer, inhaling the scent of his mate with each breath, knowing the hours they had together would pass quickly enough.

"I'm going to miss you."

"Me too." That was the understatement of the century.

Pete pressed back against him, and Tobias soaked in his heat as he listened to Pete's soft breathing even out and turn to gentle snores. Tobias had no idea how long he lay in the darkness, his eyes closed, listening, breathing, smelling, and taking in the last few hours he'd have his mate with him. Time ticked away, and eventually Tobias fell asleep, even though he wanted to make the most of every minute he had.

MORNING CAME too quickly, and so did Pete's packing and saying good-bye to everyone. There were tears from Pete and Clarie. Even Lorraine seemed misty-eyed and handed Pete little Edward to hold and say good-bye to.

"You're going to grow up big and strong like your uncle." Pete turned away and lowered his head to Edward's. Even Tobias's wolf hearing couldn't pick up what Pete said at first. "Be good always, okay? You are special… always know that." Pete handed Edward back to Lorraine, and Tobias turned away as Pete said his last farewells.

Tobias led Pete to the truck and got him and his things inside. The clouds hung low and rain began falling just as Tobias started the engine for the two-hour drive to where Pete was supposed to meet his group. Tobias didn't know what to say, and the trip was difficult because of the weather, so they pretty much sat quietly while he drove.

The miles fell away under the tires and Tobias wished for a blowout or something just so he could spend a few extra minutes with his mate. But he rarely got exactly what he wanted, and Tobias drove his truck into the park and to the lot where dozens of buses sat waiting for their passengers. One of those buses was going to take Pete away. He suddenly hated the sight of all of them and turned away to find a place to park.

This was it. The moment they'd been rushing toward ever since Pete had shown up on his pack land and the minute Tobias had dreaded but had known would come. The last few minutes he'd ever see his mate.

CHAPTER 9

PETE SAT in the truck, reluctant to open the door. As they'd driven, the clouds had gotten lower and the rain heavier until it poured down outside, echoing Pete's feelings. It truly was time for him to go home. He knew that, as much as he liked and cared for everyone in the pack, even Lorraine, he didn't belong here. Pete wasn't sure what to say. The only things that came to mind sounded like lines from stupid movies, and this felt like it deserved something better than that.

"Pete," Tobias breathed, and Pete turned away from the door. Tobias gently slipped his hand around the back of his neck, drew him closer, and kissed him. This was no gentle peck, but a deep, hard, soul-wrapping kiss that made Pete ache for more. He moaned softly and returned every searing second of it. He slid across the bench seat until he held Tobias tight. Pete was going to remember this for the rest of his life. When they separated, every second of that kiss had been etched so deeply into his brain that Pete was sure when he was eighty, he'd be able to recall every single twitch of Tobias's lips.

"I should go." Lingering was not going to make any of this easier and would only prolong the ache.

"You take care." Tobias pressed a scrap of paper into his hand. "This is my e-mail address."

Pete took the scrap and put it into his wallet so he wouldn't lose it. Then he kissed Tobias once again before opening the door. The rain had let up a little, but thunder rolled around them, and Pete closed the door and hurried under the shelter, where groups were lining up to board their buses. It took him a minute to find his. The leader scowled when he saw Pete, who ignored him and joined the others. He didn't care what the idiot thought.

"Are you okay?" Lisa, the woman ahead of him in line, asked. "They told us you were okay and that you'd gotten lost but had found your way back on your own. I'm sorry that happened to you. It must have ruined your vacation."

Pete didn't hesitate for a second and shook his head. "Lisa, I had the time of my life, and if I had it to do all over again, I'd get just as lost." He looked across the parking lot and saw Tobias standing behind his truck, watching him, water dripping off his soaked clothes.

Lisa followed his gaze. "Is that the man who found you?"

Pete nodded. "Yeah."

"Then, honey, for him, I'd get lost too."

The words barely registered as the line began to move, and Pete followed Lisa, only half paying attention as he continued watching Tobias. The rain beat down and Pete didn't notice. Water dripped from his hair and ran down his face, but he still stopped at the door of the bus for a final look before climbing inside.

"You might want to change," the leader said when Pete reached the top of the stairs and realized he was soaked through. Pete hurried back to the bathroom and changed into dry clothes from his pack, wrung out the wet ones, and stuffed them into a plastic bag. When he returned to his seat, Pete looked out the rain-streaked window for Tobias or the truck, but the spot was empty.

The bus engine started and it moved forward. The air was stifling from the damp and dozens of people, so he cracked his window for some fresh air as the bus pulled out of the lot and onto the road, to take him to the airport and home.

The ventilation finally made an appearance, and Pete was about to put the window up when he heard it—a low cry that touched him deep inside.

"Hey, that's a wolf," the man in the seat next to him said.

The driver pulled to a stop and everyone lowered their windows. The guide began explaining about wolf cries and what they could mean and some shit that didn't mean anything at all, because Pete knew what that cry meant. It was *his* wolf out there, alone, and that was the cry of loss. The long, low rumble of a single, wolf voice echoed over the land and into the bus and settled deep into Pete's heart.

"Isn't that beautiful?" the woman behind him asked. "And to think we got to hear it."

"I wonder what this one means?" the man next to her asked as Pete heard the window raise and click into place.

Pete was well aware of the loss, hurt, pain, and loneliness that cry meant; he felt that same thing deep in the pit of his stomach. The others raised their windows, but Pete stayed close to his as the bus pulled forward. Another cry reached his ears, and that was the last he heard of Tobias. With tears filling his eyes, Pete pushed the window back into place, settled in his seat, and turned toward the glass so no one would see the tears as they ran down his face.

AFTER WHAT seemed like days—well, he guessed it was a full day since he'd left Wyoming—several long bus rides, delayed flights, and missed connections all meant he arrived in New York at the tiny apartment he shared with Roger a little after nine in the morning. Pete trudged into the building and then to the elevator, hoping the damn cranky thing worked because he didn't want to walk up eight flights of stairs with his pack. He was tired of the thing and wanted a shower, a huge meal, and then his bed.

The elevator doors slid open, and he trundled inside and pressed the button for his floor. The thing rose and the doors slid open exactly where they should. Making his way down the hall, Pete saw the door open and his friend Carter came out.

"Is he still sick?" Pete asked.

"Yes. He has bouts of energy and then severe lethargy. He's improving, but it's still going to take some time before he feels better." Carter helped him inside and closed the door. The apartment was basically four rooms: a living room/kitchen combination, a shared bathroom, and two tiny bedrooms. The door to Roger's was closed. "He'll want to talk to you. I'm sure he'll be awake in a few hours. The doctor said his was a mild case, and they expect him to be up and around again soon."

"I was talking to him a few days ago and he sounded pretty good."

"That's the thing." Carter sat on the sofa, and Pete took the old chair he'd rescued from a moving sale. The fabric was tatty, but he'd gotten a blue throw to put over it, and the chair was übercomfortable. "He overdid it and now he's really tired again." Carter's eyes drifted closed.

"Okay. Have you been here the entire time I was gone?"

"Pretty much. You know him—he's such a huge baby when he's sick."

Pete groaned. "Don't I know it. You can go home if you like. I'm sure you've had about enough of His Highness in there."

"Actually he's been better than usual, and Milo has a new boyfriend, so my place has been filled with the call of the wild, if you know what I mean. God, he never quits, and I swear he goes through so many guys because he just wears them out."

Pete was too tired to do more than smile. "You know you're welcome here." He hefted himself out of the chair. "I'm going to get cleaned up and then see what I can find to eat." After that, it was sleep, and he hoped he was tired enough not to dream about a certain man.

"So Roger said you met a hot dreamboat in the wilderness. Was he a rugged, mountain-man bear?" Carter had a thing for beefy men. He always had.

"No. Tobias is tall, strong, and kind of lean, like some of those guys at the gym, except what he has comes from hard work." Pete didn't want to talk about Tobias. It brought everything from the last few days right to the front of his mind, and it was best if he just tried to forget. "He was a really nice man, and I liked him a lot."

"Did he show you what those wild men are like?"

"God, Carter, get your mind out of the gutter. Tobias was a good guy and he helped me out." He schooled his face but not in time. Carter could always read people so damn well.

"You fell in love with the guy, didn't you?" Carter jumped to his feet and was right there, hugging him tight. "That must have been something if you could feel this way after just three days."

"We're from two different worlds, and it was time I came home."

146

"Are you crazy?" Carter asked, still holding him tight. "He's a guy and so are you. It isn't like you're separate species or something. You could have figured something out if you wanted to. I mean, you want to write, and the last time I checked, the stuff you need to do that is pretty portable."

Pete kept quiet about the whole species comment. "It was only three days." He returned Carter's hug, then released him after a short while. "I'm probably just overtired and cranky. I'll feel better once I get something to eat and can sleep for a while." He picked up his luggage and left the room.

His bedroom looked the same, and Pete unpacked his bags. He hung up his wet clothes to dry and then took a quick shower. Sweats and a T-shirt never felt so good. He raided the refrigerator and then climbed into bed and fell asleep as soon as his head hit the pillow.

He didn't get his wish. Pete dreamed of Tobias, dreamed of being held tightly in strong arms, with Tobias growling softly from behind him. Pete rolled over, and they were face-to-face, looking into each other's eyes, and then he was pulled close. Everything seemed so real; each scent and touch was like Tobias was in bed with him. Tobias leaning over him, looking into his eyes, entering him with such force that took his breath away. Pete groaned and held on, making love to the man of his dreams in his dreams.

He started awake, sitting up, looking for Tobias, but of course he wasn't there.

"Are you okay?" Carter asked, sticking his head inside the cracked-open door. "I heard yelling."

"I'm fine." Pete hoped he sounded normal and not like he'd just had a huge disappointment. "I'll be out soon." He rubbed his eyes, hoping to clear away the residual sleep. "Is Roger still asleep?"

"I think I heard him trying to get up."

Pete nodded, pushed back the covers, and slowly got out of bed as Carter left, closing the bedroom door. Pete was starving and went right to the kitchen to see what was in the house for dinner. He found some pasta and the makings for sauce and got to work.

147

"So you're back." Roger shuffled in, wearing a pair of Pokémon pajamas. "I'd hug you, but I have to be careful not to spread this crap." He smiled and sat on one end of the sofa. "The cupboard farthest from the stove has the dishes I've been using. I don't want to pass this on to anyone, so we've been keeping them separated."

"Okay."

"Hopefully I'm getting better and this whole ordeal will be over soon. But apparently I have to be careful around other people for a while yet." He sat back and seemed drained of energy. "How was the trip?"

"It was fine."

Carter came in the kitchen and poured a glass of water that he brought to Roger, and then he sat in the chair. "That's not what you said to me." Carter could be such a gossip.

"I know all about you getting lost and being rescued by a wildwood hunk."

"It was more than that, okay? I spent three days with his entire family." That was the best way he could describe it so they'd understand. "His sister had a baby while I was there, and I got to hold him." How could he possibly describe the feeling of belonging he got from them when he'd rarely felt as though he belonged anywhere? "His mom really liked me, and we helped each other cook."

"You really liked them too, didn't you?"

"Yeah, I did."

"So why didn't you stay?" Roger asked. "Here you're a waiter and you live in a tiny apartment with me."

"I don't belong there. They live off the land, and…." His answer sounded hollow. The truth was, Tobias hadn't exactly asked him to stay, and Pete wasn't going to force himself on anyone. He'd learned to be independent and strong when he was in the foster care system, and he'd be damned if he was going to stay where he wasn't invited. "It just didn't work out, and besides, it was only three damn days. Who pulls up roots and moves across the country because they met a guy four—no, I guess it's five—days ago?" He hoped that sounded logical. It did to him. "It was an interesting adventure, but I'm home now and it's over." Pete got the sauce simmering before approaching Roger. "If you ever book us on some rustic adventure vacation again, where I have to spend days in the woods, so help me God—" Roger flinched, and Pete grinned. "—I'll go with you, because I had the time of my life."

"Well, that's good to know." Roger relaxed. "I thought you were going to hit me."

"When I was wandering the woods after dark, alone, and thought I was going to die, I swore if I did, that I'd come back and haunt you for the rest of your life. I swear to God I cursed you every which way possible, especially after I was attacked by a cougar."

"You're like Supergayboy," Carter interjected.

"But I found shelter and everything worked out. I'm not dead, so I'm not going to haunt you. At least for now." Pete patted Roger's shoulder and then returned to the kitchen to finish making dinner. "So what's been happening here besides you getting over your mono?"

Carter started in telling him all about their friends and the messes they'd gotten into. "Virginia went out with this girl from Brooklyn, Sally or something like that. Apparently they met at a Weight Watchers meeting and they have been happily watching each other's weight since you left." Carter seemed proud of his witticism. "I know, I'm being catty and need a saucer of milk. They seem happy and good for each other. You know Virginia's always so conscious of how she looked and tried every diet known to womankind…."

Pete did because she talked about them all the time.

"Well, it seems all she really needed was to fall in love. She's happy, and all kidding aside, I think they're perfect for each other," Carter added.

"Apparently Rodney hooked up with some guy at a club and caught a case of little crotch creatures. So he made a stop at the clinic to get them taken care of." Roger closed his eyes. "I think I'm done with the bars. We never meet anyone there other than guys who want to fuck, and let's face it, we aren't going to be young and cute forever. So between naps, I've been thinking we should join some organizations or something. Meet people who want more out of life."

"You mean like go to church?" Carter asked. "I gave up church for Lent years ago, and it was the best thing that ever happened to me."

"Not church." Roger leaned back. "I mean something fun that we can do together and maybe meet some people who are interested in more than just fucking… and then being gone the next morning." He sighed. "There has to be more to life than just night after night of playing around."

"What brought this on?" Carter asked, leaning forward a little.

"I've just had plenty of time to think, and I want more than that. Maybe I'm getting older—God knows I'm not getting smarter—but something needs to change."

"I think you're right," Pete agreed halfheartedly. It wasn't as though he disagreed with Roger, but he wasn't up to feeling excited about anything at the moment. "Maybe I'll join a cooking club or something." He tasted the sauce and put the pasta on and began making some quick garlic bread. Pete wasn't sure how much food Roger would want, but he made plenty for leftovers, regardless.

Once he was done, Pete got three plates, dished them up, and handed them out, using the ones for Roger that he'd specified.

It was nice have dinner with his friends the way he used to, and they ate in relative contented quiet. But partway through the meal, he couldn't help wondering what Tobias and his pack were up to. Their meals were always loud and filled with family being family. They teased and joked with each other. They had been a large family, even the guys from the other pack, and Pete had felt privileged to be part of it, even for only a few days.

Pete shook his head after a few seconds, pulling his attention to the present. It didn't matter what was happening back with the pack. He was here, back home, and it was best if he simply forgot what had happened and moved on. Tobias was wonderful, but he needed to let him become a nice memory and nothing more.

"Where are you?" Carter asked, and Pete realized he'd been woolgathering and hadn't heard a word of what they'd said.

"Sorry." Pete did his best to pay attention for the rest of the meal and then cleaned up when they were done. Carter went home, and Pete put Roger to bed. Once the apartment was quiet, Pete finished unpacking and came across the impressions he'd written while sitting in the glen with Tobias. He picked up his old laptop from the dresser in his room and took them to the living room. Pete meant to transcribe them into a file, but a story began to take shape and he started writing instead.

"PETE, YOU'RE going to be late for work," Roger said as he came into the living room. "You were out here all night?"

Pete cracked his eyes open and stretched his aching back. "I got an idea for a story and I wanted to get started." Thankfully he'd saved the file. He checked the time and snapped the lid on his laptop closed before jumping up and hurrying to his room. He needed to get changed and hurry down to the restaurant or he wasn't going to have a job.

After rushing the eight blocks to work, he arrived just in time and went right to it. Once his shift was done, he collected his tips, hurried back to the apartment, and got back to writing. During his shift, the entire story he wanted to tell had taken form, laid out like an intricate roadmap in front of him.

For days, Pete poured everything he had into it, then went to bed each night to dream of what was to come, went to work, and then wrote what he'd dreamed.

"You need to stop and rest," Roger scolded almost a week later.

Pete shook his head and continued working. If he stopped, the story might cease flowing, and that would be worse than anything else. He was getting close and needed to finish. Nothing else mattered at the moment. It was like his soul demanded he write his story—well, his and Tobias's story. At least that was where it started and what he'd originally envisioned, but as he worked, the story

151

unfolded and got larger, more involved, with ideas coming at him from every direction.

Nearly a month after he came home, he wrote the last words and saved the file to his computer for the last time. It was nearly two in the morning, and he wished he had someone to share his accomplishment with, but Roger was in bed and it was too late to call Carter. In the end he sent a note to Tobias to tell him what he'd done and then made a PDF of the file and sent it to him as well with a note explaining the inspiration for the story. Then he went to bed and once again dreamed of Tobias.

Before his visit to the pack, his dreams had always been relatively flat, but since returning, they had been vivid and usually of Tobias. In his dreams Tobias was so real and always made him feel special and more alive than Pete felt when he was awake. The things Tobias did to him and made him feel…. Each morning when he woke, it was like his body went back to sleep as he faced his mundane days.

"You know, you need to figure out what you really want," Roger told him the morning after he'd finished his manuscript. "All you've done is work for weeks now. The restaurant, your story— that's all you've lived for. I've been here, but you've barely noticed me at all."

"I'm sorry, I—"

"You have nothing to be sorry for. But I know you haven't been happy. Well, except when you've been writing, existing in your own imagination. Then it's like you don't want to rejoin the rest of us. Everything is perfect for you in this world you've created."

"Is there anything wrong with that?" Pete challenged.

"No. It's fine, and it's what will make you a great storyteller. But it isn't happiness. You should have that in the real world, not just in your head. So I'll say it again: you need to decide what you want."

"I'm fine," Pete groaned and leaned back.

"No, you're not. You're existing and little else. And don't think I haven't figured out what's got you so distracted even when you aren't working." Roger sat next to him. "You know, it's okay to miss him. It doesn't matter if you knew him three days or three years. You fell in love with him."

"Okay, I did. But what do I do now?"

Roger didn't seem to have any more answers than he did. "Telling you to get over him and move on isn't going to do you any good. You already know what you need to do, but it hasn't happened. We all can see that. You knew the guy for less than a week, and you've been back a month, but you still miss him." Roger leaned forward to look in his eyes. "Is this some infatuation because you're remembering how happy you were there?"

"No. It's more than that. Last week when I got that great tip from the mayor when he was sitting at my table in the restaurant, I went back to the kitchen and wanted to tell Tobias all about it. I know it's dumb-sounding, but I feel like he's here with me, and...."

Roger squeezed his hand a little tighter. "Okay. So you truly love the guy."

"I know it sounds completely stupid."

"Maybe. But there is one question you have to answer." Roger tilted his head to the side slightly, raising one eyebrow upward. Pete knew that look; he'd seen it before. It was Roger's "get over it" look. "What the hell are you going to do about it?"

Chapter 10

"If you don't stop moping, I'm going to hit you with this pan!" Clarie's eyes blazed and then her expression softened. "I tried to tell you how hard this was going to be on you, but you didn't want to hear it."

"Mom, he's gone and has been for a month."

"That doesn't matter and you know it. He's still your mate. You're going to miss him, and there will always be part of you that will feel empty." She set the pan on the stove and walked around to where he stood on the other side of the counter. "But it isn't his fault."

"I know."

His mother pointed out the window. "You have the entire pack walking on eggshells. They feel the tension that's building and churning inside you. We all can."

"I haven't said a word to anyone about it."

"No, you haven't. But you don't smile any longer, and there's no happiness in anything you do. Winter is coming, and you have everything ready because you always do. You take care of all of us, but you used to laugh and joke. Have you noticed that Greg is once again sleeping in the woods away from everyone?"

"Why?" Tobias had to admit that he hadn't noticed, and that bothered him.

"I don't know. Why don't you ask him?"

"Because you tend to know just about everything that's going on." Damn, that sounded whiny even to his own ears. His mother was right. He'd been doing what he needed to and basically keeping to himself, which was not good for a leader or the pack. Tobias sat on one of the stools as realization hit him. Zev had said he wanted to take Tobias's pack, but Tobias had himself done what Zev couldn't. In a way, he'd given up his pack when he sent Pete away, or at least he'd abdicated his leadership.

"Don't give me that attitude. Your pack needs you, and they need all of you."

"I know." He felt like crap and had ever since he'd watched Pete ride away on that bus. "What do I do?"

"I don't have any answers for you." She gently patted his shoulder. "That has to come from you. It would be a start if you went and found out what was going on. Talk to the pack and make them realize that they do have a leader who cares for them. They've been ignored, and we've been lucky that nothing has arisen, but you know that isn't going to continue."

"I know, Mom. It's just that it's...."

She stepped back. "You need to remember that you made your own decision and now you need to live with it and all its consequences. But it isn't fair to make the rest of the pack pay for it."

Tobias patted the counter lightly and stood. "You're right." He walked to his mother and gently hugged her. She seemed surprised but then returned his hug. "It's time I returned to the land of the living." He released her, left the house, and walked down to where the others were working to get wood in for the winter.

Tobias joined in the production, helping to stack the wood on the growing pile.

"Where's Greg?" he asked Brick.

"He's been spending his time in the woods again." Brick lifted his axe and split the log cleanly before reaching for another. "I think he misses Pete. There was something about him that brought Greg out of his shell. He was always so happy and full of energy." He swung the axe once again, and the split log went flying in both directions.

"Yeah, he was," Hayden agreed, and Sasha and Ryan both nodded.

"We all miss him." Ryan stepped closer, and Tobias let him lead him away from the others. "We all know what Pete is to you. Far be it from us to question what you think is best, but do you think you did the right thing?"

"I didn't have much of a choice."

Ryan hesitated, then turned away and took a step back toward the others before spinning around once again. "We always have a choice. Sometimes we make the right one and sometimes we make a mistake. Your father once told me that what made a great leader was the ability to see when he'd made a mistake and fix it."

"I don't know if I can." Tobias smiled, walked to Ryan, and put an arm around his shoulder. "But I can work on making things better for all of us here." He was about to turn away and stopped. Ryan had been his friend for many years, and even so, he hesitated to talk about what was truly bothering him. Tobias had to give Ryan credit—he was patient and waited.

"Maybe you should ask the Mother."

"No. She already gave me her answer and even told me what she expected me to do. I… I followed what I felt was best and ignored her advice. I don't think she's going to be eager to talk with me right now."

"You could mate with another. Then the imprint from Pete would be gone and you could move on."

"No, I can't do that to someone else. I found my true mate and I let him go. I have to live with that for the rest of my life, and there's nothing I can do about it."

"Can I ask something?" Ryan waited as Tobias nodded slowly. "Have you been sleeping?" Sometimes Ryan saw so much more than Tobias meant him to. "Or dreaming?"

"Yes." He'd been dreaming of Pete every night. He was with him then, and the few minutes after waking was the only time the ache in his heart receded. Tobias closed his eyes and could see Pete standing in front of him, smiling wickedly, eyes gleaming, as the sun shone on his glistening skin after they'd swum in the creek. His body reacted, and Tobias lifted his hand to touch him. Of course, it was just a daydream and Pete vanished into mist. Tobias was once again alone, and his heart hurt like there was a hole in it.

"We can take care of things here," Ryan offered, and Tobias nodded and left the men to their work, his burst of energy having passed.

His mother was right. He needed to do something, because all he could think about was Pete and it was driving him crazy. Tobias entered the cabin the pack had built for Sasha and Lorraine and found his sister sitting in a chair, bouncing Edward gently on her shoulder.

"It's good to see you," she said, all smiles.

"He's growing quickly."

"Yes. Eddie's a strong one. I think he's going to take after you."

"I don't feel so strong now."

"Horseshit," Lorraine countered. "Heartache visits everyone. It doesn't know any difference, and it sneaks under all our defenses."

"Mom says I need to do something about it."

"She's usually right." Lorraine gently moved the baby off her shoulder and placed him in Tobias's arms. "Look into those eyes and that face. He's happy and content and knows all he needs to of his world at the moment. He eats when he's hungry, is changed and held, and sleeps. Everything he could need. Then he'll grow up, and he'll learn to do without and strive to get what he wants. We never have it all again."

"Since when did you get to be such a philosopher?"

"I don't know. He's opened my eyes to so many things." Lorraine stood in front of Tobias, her dark, penetrating eyes looking deep into his soul. "You deserve to be happy."

"Yes, I do. But so does Pete." Tobias looked down at the sleeping baby and smiled. "You are an amazing little one, you know that, pup?"

Edward yawned and crinkled his face before settling once again.

"And you're a good leader. But I want you to do something for me and all of us. If you sent Pete away because you thought we'd be safer or because you think he's happier going home, I think you're wrong on both counts. All of us could see how much he cared for you."

"Yes. I know he did. But do you think this is enough for him after living all those years in the city?"

Lorraine shook her head. "Are you worried Pete won't fit into the pack and that we won't be enough for him? Or that *you* won't be enough?" Her gaze was piercing, and Tobias growled at the way she stood up to him. Lorraine backed down and tilted her head to the side to show she knew her place. "I'm only telling you the truth. Besides, if you want my opinion, I think you're everything he wants."

"Then why didn't he stay?" Tobias asked.

Edward began to fuss, so Lorraine lifted him from Tobias's arms. "Did you ask him to?" She turned as Edward's fussing continued and took him into the other room to change him.

Tobias didn't answer her question and instead told her he'd see her and Edward at dinner and left her to take care of him. He was at loose ends and figured he might as well catch up on pack business and make sure they had enough supplies and resources to get through the winter.

His office was small and utilitarian. Tobias woke up his computer and logged on to check the various pack accounts. Everything was as it should be, and he printed the latest statements for review and then opened his e-mail. There were only a few, and one was from Pete with a file attached.

> *Tobias*
> *I kept thinking of you and everyone there. You all inspired this story. Everyone there made a wonderful impression on me, and I wanted to both say thank you to them and show you personally how you affected me. I hope you like it.*
> *Pete*

Tobias clicked open the file. He thought of printing it out but began reading instead. He sat enthralled, unable to turn away for hours, and it wasn't until he reached the end of Pete's story that he looked up from the screen, mouth hanging open. He'd missed so much when Pete was here. The way he'd described the meadow, the creek, and even him, had been filled with such love. The sense of family Pete had created in the story and how the main character had come to find in the pack the one thing he'd always wanted and hadn't had—that had to have come directly from Pete's own longings. There was no other way he could have written so movingly. And Tobias had ignored that when Pete had been here. He'd been so wrapped up in what he thought was right for Pete he'd neglected everything Pete wanted most. Well, that wasn't true—he hadn't missed everything. What he hadn't understood was the intensity.

Tobias wiped his eyes and closed the file. "Goddammit," he said out loud as the loss he kept at bay most of the time washed over him yet again. It was his own fault.

Tobias was about to turn off the computer when the icon changed to show he had another e-mail. He opened it and felt the blood drain from his face.

"Mom, Ryan, Sasha!" Tobias yelled loud enough to rattle the windows, and footsteps raced toward the room. "Ryan, you're in charge while I'm gone. Sasha, get on this computer and get me on the first plane to New York. I'm going to pack."

"Why?" his mother asked.

"You know how we haven't seen Zev in a month? Well, Pete found him. He's in New York, and Pete thinks he's being stalked. I have to go and put an end to this." He also needed to go get his mate back.

His mother hurried away.

"I'll go find Brick so he can drive you to the airport," Ryan said and followed her out.

Tobias backed away from the computer, and Sasha got to work. "There's a flight that leaves from Cheyenne in six hours. It goes through Minneapolis and gets you into New York tomorrow morning. I'm booking you a seat now, but you need to leave in fifteen minutes to make sure you get there in time. Should I answer the e-mail and tell Pete you're on your way?"

"Yes, and try to get me an address where I can find him."

Ryan had already left to find Brick, and Tobias hurried to find his mother and finish packing. By the time he carried the old suitcase to the living room, the entire pack had gathered to say good-bye. Sasha handed him paperwork with his flight information, as well as an e-mail printout from Pete. Brick had truck keys and was ready to go.

"I'll take care of everything here. You go protect and bring back your mate." Ryan hugged him and then backed away.

Greg was there in human form, and they shared a hug as well. The rest of the pack said their good-byes, and he hugged his mother before hurrying out to the truck.

Tobias put his bag behind the seat, waited for Brick to hop in, and drove as quickly as he dared until he reached the pavement. Then he sped up, and after he reached the highway, Tobias grew more and more nervous by the second.

He reached the airport in Cheyenne two hours before his flight was scheduled to take off. Tobias pulled up and unloaded his things, then turned to Brick, who seemed just as nervous as he was. "You can get a hotel if you want." Tobias's offer was met by Brick shaking his head. It was the reaction he expected. Wolves didn't do well in cities, and while Cheyenne wasn't large by any means, there was too much activity for Brick. "Then drive back carefully and take your time." He pulled him into a hug. "I'll be back as soon as I can, and please help Ryan take care of the others."

"Greg hates me." Brick had been silent for hours and now he decided to say something.

"I'm sure he doesn't."

"He wants something I can't give him. Greg's not my mate, but he wants to be my mate."

Tobias couldn't believe the timing of the conversation he was having. "Just tell him how you feel. That he isn't your mate and that he'll know for sure when he meets him, just as you will when you meet her. Tell him that Mikael is planning to have a pack gathering and that we'll be going. It will be a chance for packs to meet one another and for mates to find each other. The entire pack won't come, but I'll bring both of you and hopefully you'll both find what you need." In their small group, there was little chance to meet others.

"Okay." Brick seemed less edgy.

"You could have told me this on the drive."

Brick nodded but didn't say anything more.

"Just be Greg's friend and pack brother. That's what he needs more than anything. He's having a hard time because he wants to find his mate so badly."

"Okay."

Tobias handed Brick the keys and watched as he got into the truck and slowly drove away. Tobias said a short prayer to the Mother to watch over Brick on the drive home and the rest of his pack while he was gone. Then he hefted his suitcase and made his way inside.

TOBIAS'S SENSES were on overdrive by the time he landed in New York. A flight delay had had his wolf pacing for hours. Everywhere he turned for the last day, something assaulted his ears, nose, or taste, and all the people crammed into the airplanes was enough to make him ill, with their scents overlapping on top of one another. And the airports with their cleaning chemicals, burned food, and the bathrooms that nearly made him sick, not to mention the scent of jet fuel and exhaust that burned his nose almost constantly. Then there was the constant scream of engines and dozens of conversations all happening at once in a confined space. When he got off the last plane in Newark and into the airport, he thought his head was going to explode from the sensory overload.

Tobias pulled out his very old cell phone, half surprised it still worked. Pete had given him a phone number, and Tobias called it but got a recording.

"Can I help you?" a man pulling a luggage cart asked after nearly running into him.

"I need to get here." Tobias showed the man the printout he had from Pete.

"The taxi stand is just down the way."

Tobias thanked him and hurried to where he indicated. His agitation increased when he had to wait in line, with people jostling him and his wolf screaming to get out and defend itself from the

161

onslaught. He finally made it to the front of the line and gave the driver the address.

He was getting closer to Pete, and his wolf paced faster and faster. His mate was near, and nothing was going to stop him this time.

It took a while and almost all of Tobias's cash, but he stood in front of Pete's building. Even over the nose-wrinkling smell of the city, he scented Pete, but as he climbed the steps and went inside, he knew Zev had been here as well, his acrid scent permeating through everything else. It was hard for him to judge just how recently Zev had been inside. Tobias's footsteps echoed in the stairwell, and he picked up his pace the higher he got. At the eighth floor, he pushed open the door. Pete's scent was even stronger, cutting through those of the other people who lived here. He didn't need to check the numbers to know which apartment he needed—his nose led him right to it, and Tobias pounded on the door.

"It's so early," he heard inside but not from Pete.

"I'm coming." That was Pete, and as soon as the door opened, Tobias dropped what he held, pulled Pete into his arms, and hugged him as tightly as he could while he buried his face in his neck and inhaled his scent just to make sure it was really him. Tobias carded his fingers through Pete's silky hair, hardly able to believe he had his mate in his arms once again.

"You're here."

"Did you get my note?" Tobias asked without moving. He wasn't letting anything come between them again. "Yes, I came. You asked for help and I'm here." Tobias shook as his wolf lurked just under the surface. He pressed them both inside the apartment and moved to kick the door closed.

"Dude, this New York," Pete said and brushed by him, quickly grabbed the suitcase, and hauled it inside, then closed and locked the door.

Tobias grunted without turning away from Pete. That was as close to a thank-you as he could manage at the moment. He pulled Pete close enough to bring their lips together, claiming them in a voracious kiss. Pete wrapped his arms around Tobias's neck, held on to him, and returned the kiss.

"Okay, you two might want to take this someplace else. Because as hot as this is, it only reminds me how long it's been since I've gotten some."

"Hmmm," Pete mumbled against Tobias's lips and eventually pulled away. "Ummm...." He didn't turn away. "Roger, this is Tobias." He smiled, and Tobias kissed him once again, just because Pete was too close not to.

"I guessed that," Roger said with a snicker, and Tobias growled at him.

"Don't. Roger is my roommate." Pete released him and stepped back.

Tobias reluctantly let Pete go and extended his hand. Roger took it, and when he did, Tobias leaned in.

"Are you smelling me?" Roger released his hand and backed away.

Tobias didn't answer, but he filed away his impressions for later. Roger was an interesting man, and he needed to think on him for a while.

"We should talk," Tobias said to Pete, looking around, then smelled his way to Pete's bedroom. They entered, and Tobias closed the door behind them. He could barely believe he had Pete alone once again.

"You said you wanted to talk." Pete's prompt pulled Tobias out of his mating-lust haze, but it was hard for him to get his thoughts straight. "Okay. Let's start with Zev."

"Let's start with the fact that I never should have let you go." Tobias pulled Pete to him and had every intention of pressing him back onto the bed, stripping him bare, and making sure that no one had touched his mate while they were apart. His wolf was very close to the surface and demanding control.

"Tobias."

"No, I should have asked you to stay and then begged you if you said no. Letting you leave was the worst mistake I've ever made. You're my mate, the only one I get, and I've been miserable without you." He lifted Pete off his feet and set him on the bed. He could hold off no more. Everything else could wait until he'd been with his mate once again.

Tobias tugged at Pete's shoes and then his shirt and pants, stripped him completely, and then pulled off his own clothes in record time. "If you don't want this, say so now, because I'm not going to have much control."

"Oh God." Pete pulled him down, and Tobias claimed his lips and ran his hands down Pete's smooth body, feeling him all over to reacquaint himself with every inch of him.

"Guys!" a voice called from outside the door.

"Go away!" Tobias snapped. He slid down between Pete's legs and took his cock deep into his throat. Pete groaned loudly as Tobias tasted his mate in the best way possible. This was his Pete, and damn if he didn't taste like heaven.

"Uh, guys…."

Roger was certainly persistent. Tobias sucked harder, and Pete moaned louder. Thankfully there was no more interruption as Tobias sucked a writhing, moaning Pete to near oblivion. Damn, this was paradise, and as Pete got closer to the edge, Tobias sucked him even harder until Pete's salty sweetness burst on his tongue and Tobias reached his own climax like some teenager unable to control himself. Tobias let Pete's cock slip from between his lips, his mind clouded with desire.

"Guys, now would be a good time…." Roger pounded on the door, and Tobias was ready to pound him. He stalked to it, stuck his head out, and growled deeply. "That guy is out front."

Tobias closed the door and groaned as he tossed Pete's clothes at him and began pulling on his pants. He yanked open the door and fastened his jeans as he hurried to the front window. Zev stood across the street, looking up at the apartment. "This has to end now." He turned away, and Pete handed him his shirt.

"What are you going to do?"

"What I should have done the first time."

Pete took his hand. "You can't… not here in the city."

"I have to." Tobias left the apartment, descended the stairs, and stalked through the lobby and out the front door. He put his hands on his hips and glared at Zev, who stared back, a silent battle of wills separated by the street.

"This was a mistake. You should have stayed in whatever hole you crawled into." Tobias barely spoke above a whisper, knowing Zev would hear him.

"I knew you'd come, and here, there's no pack to back you up." Zev grinned, and Tobias heard the door open behind him. He smelled Pete and was about to ask what in the hell he was doing out here when Pete moved next to him and put a single hand on his shoulder.

"I have something better than pack. I have my mate. Now, do you want to play games or do this?" He didn't look away for a second. Tobias was stronger than Zev; he could sense it. But there was part of him that was closed off, and that worried Tobias. However, there was nothing he could do about it now.

"Yes. I want it all. You'll scream for me and wish for death before I kill you, take your mate, and take your pack."

"The alley behind the building in two hours," Pete said softly from next to him.

"Fine. But bring your mate—I want to claim my prize when you lose." Zev pivoted and walked down the sidewalk, turned the corner, and disappeared from sight.

Tobias didn't move until he was sure Zev was gone, and then he took Pete's hand and led him back inside and up the stairs. "We need to talk, but…."

"Roger leaves for work in half an hour. He's a bus dispatcher for the city. We can talk then." Pete opened the apartment door, and Roger was already dressed in his uniform.

"I figured you two could use some time alone. Is that creepy guy gone?"

"Yes, and I doubt you'll be seeing him again. One way or another, this will be over in a few hours."

"O-kay?" Roger hugged Pete, sending a stab of possessive jealously racing through Tobias. Once Roger left, he relaxed.

Pete took Tobias's hand. "Okay. Here's my plan. There are dumpsters at either end of the alley that we can put across to keep cars out. There are no windows that face the alley, and currently the light outside the back door is broken, so it's as dark as a tomb. No one goes out there at night, so it should be private enough for what the two of you need to do. I was afraid that if we let Zev name a place, you'd be at a disadvantage."

"Good thinking. Now you need to get away from here and go somewhere safe."

"No." Pete put his hands on his hips, staring at him with hard eyes and tight lips. "You pushed me away before because you thought it was for my own good, and you aren't doing it again. I know what I want, and that's you. I'm your mate and you're mine. I don't know exactly what all that means, but I *do* know I intend to find out. So I'm going to be there when you challenge Zev and bring this to an end."

Tobias was too overwhelmed to oppose him. "If that's what you want." He could no longer deny his feelings or what Pete wanted.

"It is. Now let's go take a look at the alley to see if there is anything that can give you an advantage." Pete took his hand and led him out of the apartment and back down the stairs.

AFTER LOOKING at the alley and seeing that its enclosed and confined space was perfect for what they needed, he and Pete spent much of the next two hours together, making love. There was a chance he wouldn't come out of this challenge alive. Zev had something up his sleeve, and Tobias wasn't sure what it was.

"I really do want you to leave while you can." Tobias knew it was probably useless, but he wanted Pete safe more than anything.

"Not going to happen."

Pete got out of bed and began dressing. Tobias did as well, and they went downstairs and to the back of the building. They expected Zev in about ten minutes. Pete hurried to one end of the alley and tugged an empty dumpster across the entrance. Tobias did the same at the other end. Everything was in shadow now and growing darker by the second. The lights of the city blotted out the stars overhead, but on the ground, it was near pitch-black. Tobias had no trouble seeing, and they returned to the doorway, stood in the sliver of light, and waited for Zev.

A silhouette crossed the light at the north end of the alley and then morphed into a wolf as it emerged from the shadow of the dumpster. This was it.

CHAPTER 11

PETE STAYED where he was, taking Tobias's clothes as he removed them and then watching as he shifted into his wolf. Pete stroked his fur and looked deep into Tobias's eyes before standing back and letting him leave. He didn't want Tobias to. Pete knew this was a wolf thing and he had to let it happen, but his heart pounded in his chest and he was afraid he was going to be sick to his stomach. He held it together and turned out the back-hallway light behind him so he could see farther into the alley.

Tobias and Zev slowly approached each other. In the darkness they looked like huge dogs, but Pete knew exactly who was who. *Keep him safe*, he sent upward to the powers that be and then focused on where the two of them circled each other, low growls reaching his ears.

The sounds of the city receded as he waited for one of them to strike. He'd never watched anything like this before, and he gasped or held his breath when one of them leaped at the other. They were moving too fast for him to tell who was who as they mixed it up, snarling. A yip reached his ears, followed by a deep growl. "Good one, Tobias. Get him." He didn't talk very loudly, but he knew the growl and snarl that followed. Another yip, then a second, and one of the wolves leaped and the other flew through the air, landed on its side, and slid on the concrete.

A familiar pair of eyes flashed in the darkness and then turned toward the downed wolf and stalked closer. Pete wanted to cheer for Tobias but only allowed himself a smile. This wasn't over, and first blood didn't mean a winner. He didn't want to be a distraction.

Tobias got closer to Zev, who slowly rose to his feet and leaped with more force than Pete expected. Zev had been playing, and damn if he didn't rake his teeth over Tobias's side. Pete wasn't sure how badly Tobias was hurt. His fingers went to his mouth and he bit his nails as more snarls filled the alley.

Tobias countered, and Zev dodged, then attacked again. Zev was clearly losing, but Tobias couldn't seem to knock him out. Both wolves stalked each other, walking in circles, Tobias favoring his rear leg while Zev favored a front. Tobias stumbled and Zev leaped. Pete closed his eyes and then opened them again.

It was a diversion! Tobias had hold of Zev good, bit, and then tossed him aside, and Zev came to rest against the building on the far side of the alley.

Pete was pretty sure that was it, the end of all of this. He knew Tobias had beaten Zev before, and once this was all over, they could go on with their lives together.

But Zev got to his feet again.

A light shone in the darkness, a single flame that burst from Zev and sailed toward Tobias, who ducked—just in time from what Pete could see. He shook as a wave of fear washed over him. Tobias had to win. Pete couldn't bear to lose him now. The flame hit the side of the building, sputtered, and went out.

"Shit. That's not fair!"

A second light followed the first, and Tobias dodged it once again, leaping right before it passed. He knocked Zev on his side and sent him tumbling along the alley as another light sailed toward Tobias and skimmed over his back.

Tobias yowled, and the scent of burning hair filled the air.

There was a higher-pitched growl coming from where Zev got to his feet. Another light didn't come, but Pete saw Tobias was moving more slowly. Now Zev pounced, and Pete braced for his impact on Tobias, holding his breath and waiting for the final outcome.

A yowl filled the air, followed by a screech and a wheeze. One wolf was down and remained so, while the other stood over it. Pete shook as the wolf bit down and tore into the neck of the other. He turned away, not wanting to see the end of this battle and possibly the end of his mate. In the final tumble, he hadn't been able to see who was who.

The air grew silent and then filled with horns and the sound of traffic once again. Pete stilled as the surviving wolf slowly made his way over to him. He was ready to run in case it was Zev. He turned on the light inside again to cast a slight beam through the doorway and into the alley as the wolf grew closer. Then familiar eyes locked on to his and Pete rushed out to help Tobias.

He was cut up, and the burn on his back looked so painful.

"Is Zev dead?" Pete asked, and Tobias nuzzled his hand. Pete took that as a yes. He needed to help him but wasn't exactly sure how. "You need to shift."

Tobias blinked at him and collapsed onto the concrete floor.

Pete closed the back door and raced down the narrow hall to the laundry room. He found a pan in the wash tub and some old laundry that someone had left in the lost and found. Running cool water, he filled the pan and raced back. When Pete placed the soaked cloth onto Tobias's back, he flinched and sighed. Pete left it there and gently stroked Tobias's big wolfy head. "You have to shift. You told me that was how you heal, and I don't know what to do for you."

Tobias licked his hand and tried to get to his feet. Pete rinsed out the cloth and put it on Tobias's back once again, hoping it was helping.

The change from wolf to man was slow and looked very painful. Pete moved back, and after what seemed like hours of bones shifting and skin stretching, which actually took only a minute or two, Tobias lay on the floor, naked but whole, except for a large welt on his back.

"Burns are bad." Tobias sat up slowly.

"Get dressed and go on up to the apartment." Pete turned toward the door. "What do I do with him? Will he stay in wolf form?"

"Yes." Tobias gritted his teeth in pain as he pulled on his clothes. "I need to shift once again to heal this fully, but I don't have the strength right now."

"Leave the shirt off. Then it won't pull on the burn." Pete helped Tobias with his shoes and then opened the door and looked out. He had to do something with the wolf body lying in the alley and then get the dumpsters put back.

"Okay. Come on." Tobias stepped out into the humidity.

Pete propped the door open and cautiously walked to where Zev lay unmoving. When he got close, he saw how Tobias had torn out his throat, and he turned, trying not to throw up. "What do we do?"

"Back home we'd bury him and give him back to the goddess, but there's nowhere here to do that. Do you think we can get him into one of the dumpsters?" Tobias lifted Zev's hind legs, and Pete took the front. He hated doing this, but there wasn't any other choice.

They managed to lift him high enough and then let go, and Zev fell into the dumpster. Pete closed the lid and pushed it back into place.

"This doesn't feel right," he whispered. "Yeah, he was a prick, but he's still your half brother."

"I know." Tobias leaned against the building, and even in the near darkness, Pete could see how tired he was. "What do I tell my mom? I mean, I have to tell her that Zev is gone, but I can't tell her that I threw her son in the garbage."

"Then this stays between you and me. There isn't anything we can do. Zev made his choice, and do you think he would have treated you any better?" Pete stood next to Tobias and ran a hand through his hair. "If they find the body of a wolf in the city, it's going to hit the news in a huge way, and what happens if they autopsy it or something and find out that it's different?" Pete hurried inside and pulled some leftover paint and chemicals from where the landlord had stashed them in the building. He opened the top of the dumpster and dumped the contents inside, then silently closed the lid. He'd come back down and take care of it. "Let's get the other dumpster back in place and go inside."

Tobias helped him finish unblocking the alley, and then they both headed into the building and closed the door behind them. Pete led him to the elevator, and they rode up. After getting Tobias onto the sofa, he busied himself making food. He didn't know what else to do for Tobias, but feeding him seemed like a good idea.

By dinner Tobias was already looking better and his back was nearly healed. Pete got him to shift and held Tobias's wolf, resting his head on his back.

"I love you. I hope you know that. Wolf and man, you're both precious to me." He stroked Tobias's side, avoiding the last remnants of his wound. When Tobias shifted back, he dressed, and they ate a quiet dinner.

As Pete did the dishes, Tobias slid his arms around his waist and pressed his chest and hips to Pete's back and butt. "Roger interrupted us earlier, but I have you all to myself now." Tobias tugged his hands out of the water and guided him away from the sink. "The dishes can wait. I've dreamed of having you in my arms for a month."

"You have?"

"Every night."

"Me too. The dreams were so real and strong. I thought I had you with me, but then I'd wake up and you would be gone." Pete quivered, Tobias's around him activating every cell in his body.

Tobias tugged Pete's shirt out of his pants and slid his hand up Pete's belly. "I love how you feel and how you taste and smell. I could stand here and be happy just smelling you for the rest of my life." Tobias kissed the base of his neck, and Pete stretched to give him more access as tingles raced up and down his spine. He opened Pete's belt, unbuttoned his pants, and pushed them down his legs, leaving him standing bareassed in the kitchen.

"Tobias," Pete said, excited as hell and embarrassed at the same time.

"Now that's a sight." Tobias pushed up his shirt and kissed his way down Pete's back, parted his cheeks, and buried his face between them.

Pete whimpered as Tobias licked and nibbled at his opening, tongue probing. He put his hands on the counter and pushed his hips back to give Tobias better access.

"Damn, Pete…."

"What are you doing to me?" Pete breathed, lolling his head back as he tried to remain upright.

"Getting you ready."

"Here?" His head grew fuzzy and he quickly became overwhelmed.

"Yes. I want you so bad." Tobias pulled away, and Pete looked over his shoulder just in time to see Tobias strip down, and then his cock, long and thick, slid down his crease.

Pete shook like leaves in a spring breeze. "Then take me. Make me yours. I want to be your mate." He gasped as Tobias breached him and slid deeper. He wanted this so badly, and as Tobias sank into him, Tobias held him tightly, his chest to Pete's back, hips to his ass, and then moved slowly. "What do you have to do?"

"I bite you and mark you as mine."

"Will I become a shifter like you when you do that?"

"No. You'll be my mate."

"But there are all these legends."

"Mostly made up to make people scared of us." Tobias withdrew and sank back inside, clouding Pete's brain with passion. "I can change you, but I won't. Not now." Tobias snapped his hips, and Pete pushed back against him.

"Then make me your mate." He threw his head back as Tobias tweaked his nipples and drove harder and faster into him. "Yes! I want you, Tobias. Make me yours."

"You already are and always will be." Tobias slid his hands down Pete's belly, and his fingers encircled his cock.

Pete thrust in time with Tobias, sliding his cock into Tobias's hand as Tobias filled him. He needed release so bad, but he held off, tense and ready for Tobias to make him his. "Tobias!" Pete's body went into overdrive and still he waited for Tobias to act.

Tobias's heated tongue teased at his neck, and as they moved together, Pete was sure this was the prelude to what was to come. He wanted to be Tobias's mate and was ready to go home with him.

"Did you miss me?"

"Yes." Pete quivered as his knees threatened to give out. "I missed you as soon as the bus pulled away." He gasped and gritted his teeth. "I thought I'd get over you, but I didn't. I just missed you more each day…. Now do it! Make me your mate forever. It's what I want." He grew more heated as Tobias drove deeper. The head of his cock grazed past the spot deep inside and sent a cry past Pete's lips as his control broke and he clamped his eyes closed.

He remained on the edge as Tobias leaned over him, licking his neck, as his release washed over him with near blinding force. Still he waited for Tobias, who shook from behind him and drove hard one final time. His teeth broke Pete's skin as he pulsed inside him, sending Pete over the edge a second time. Pete leaned back, letting Tobias hold him, as the tension left his body and he nearly collapsed. Tobias pinned him up in place until he could get hold of the counter once more.

"I thought you wanted me as your mate."

Tobias held him tighter. "You are my mate, the only one I will ever get. And yes, I need to claim you, but I'm not going to do it here in the city surrounded by all this awfulness. I'll do it back home in the woods where it's peaceful and I can feel close to the goddess. The Mother is barely present here. There are no trees, and everything has been done to remove her."

"Okay." Pete sighed as their bodies separated, and he bent to pull up his pants. When he straightened up, Tobias lifted him into his arms and carried him into the bedroom.

"Are you sure that's what you want?" Tobias asked, laying him on the bed, staring deeply into his eyes. "I know I didn't ask you before, but I am now. I want you to come with me and be part of my pack. But this has to be your decision. I won't make it for you, which is why I didn't mark you, other than to raise enough hickeys on your neck."

Pete rubbed the tender spots, then hugged Tobias to him and licked the base of his neck and sucked up a mark of his own. "Now you belong to me too."

"I see. So that's how it's going to be." Tobias grinned.

"Yup. What's good for the goose and all that. Besides, I want everyone to know that you're mine."

"I do." Tobias pressed him back onto the mattress and proceeded to slowly ramp up the heat once again. This time, when they came together, it was deeper because he got to look into Tobias's blazing eyes and see the fire inside them that burned brightly enough to warm Pete's blood as well. He wanted to stay like this forever.

THAT NIGHT, late, once Roger was home and everything was quiet, Pete got out of bed, put on an old robe and slippers, quietly descended the stairs, and went out the back door of the building. He blocked it open a crack and walked right to the dumpster, opened the lid, lit a match, and tossed it inside. Pete was back to the door before the flames reached the top of the dumpster, burning bright and hot. Inside, he went back upstairs, closed the window, and got into bed with Tobias. He raised a silent prayer for Zev's soul and stayed awake, listening for the fire trucks, but none came.

"Where did you go?" Tobias mumbled, still mostly asleep.

"To take care of Zev. His soul is heading to the Mother now." He caressed Tobias's cheek. He would explain everything to him later. "Go back to sleep, and in the morning, we'll figure things out."

"Like what?"

Pete sighed. "Like when you're going to take me home to the pack, to our family."

Tobias rolled onto his side and spooned himself to Pete's backside. "Yes. We'll go back to our family."

Not only had Pete found someone to love and who loved him, but he'd gotten a family in the process. It was definitely time to go home.

EPILOGUE

A Little Over Two Weeks Later

SOMETIMES WHEN one desperately wants things to move quickly, everything slows down.

Tobias stayed two more days after the challenge, and then Pete took him to the airport and put him on a plane and waited until he was too far away to see any longer before finally going home. After that, it was all about finding another roommate for Roger, giving notice at his job, and selling the things he wasn't bringing with him. Everything about his life in New York was behind him. Those two weeks seemed long, but now that he thought back on it, that was a short amount of time to pack up his entire life and move it completely across the country.

What was surprising was that everything important fit in three suitcases.

"What are you thinking about?" Tobias asked as he smiled down at Pete, who sat rocking little Edward. Pete was trying not to finger the still tender mating mark on his neck that Tobias had freshened up that morning in the clearing. Pete didn't want to think about it too much because getting excited while holding a baby seemed a little squicky.

He'd told Lorraine that he'd give her and Sasha a few hours alone and had urged them to go take a walk or go for a swim before it got too cold to. He had a bottle for when Edward woke up and had been instructed on how to change a diaper, so he was all set and enjoying taking care of their nephew.

It was made very clear to him when he returned that he was Uncle Pete from now on. He'd smiled when Sasha and Lorraine had

176

told him, and last night he'd held Tobias and cried for his family, the one that had been gone for so many years.

"Nothing important." Pete smiled down at Edward and then up at Tobias. He was well and truly happy, content, and in love all at the same time for the first time in his life.

"The men are building a fire for tonight, and Mom is cooking up a storm." Tobias grinned, and Pete nodded, the new mating mark on his neck pulling slightly. "Last night was just you and me. Tonight it's the entire pack's turn to welcome you and celebrate our official mating." Tobias leaned closer still. His breath caressed Pete's ear. "Then afterward you and I will have a little party of our own."

"In the bed this time?" Pete had enjoyed spending the night outside under the stars in the meadow, just the two of them. Tobias had mated him, showing him what he meant to him and giving him a glimpse of the life they hoped to have together.

"If you like." Tobias winked, and Pete wasn't so sure they'd make it to bed, but he really didn't mind. The truth was he'd follow Tobias wherever he wanted to lead them. "Have you talked to Roger?"

"I e-mailed him. He says he wants to come visit, but I haven't said anything because I don't know if that's a good idea or not."

Tobias looked at Greg, who sat quietly at the counter, head on his hand, staring out the window, most likely at nothing. "Invite him. It may do us all a world of good."

Pete narrowed his gaze. "What do you know?"

Tobias shrugged. "Alpha intuition."

"Yeah, so what does this alpha intuition say about my book?" Pete had worked extensively on his manuscript before leaving and had taken a chance by submitting it to an agent as well as a publisher. Now all he had to do was wait and see.

"My intuition tells me it's going to be accepted and a huge hit. The author is particularly brilliant." He leaned down, and Pete kissed him.

"But you're not biased." Pete wriggled his eyebrows.

"Nope." Tobias took one more kiss and then left him with Edward, who seemed ready to wake up.

Pete stood carefully and got the bottle. He gave it to him after the first cry, and Edward settled right back down, eating happily.

He sat and rocked Edward until his parents' return, smiling and much less stressed. He gently handed Lorraine her son and kissed her cheek before going to his room to change for this gathering tonight and whatever it was going to entail.

"GOOD EVENING, all. Tonight we welcome two members into our pack. Edward and Pete have joined our group, and they become part of our family."

A cheer went up from everyone. Edward fussed, and Lorraine soothed him until it was time to hand him over to Pete, who rocked him in his arms.

"Do you, Pete, promise to support your pack members to the best of your ability?" Tobias asked.

"I do, and I think this little one does too." Pete grinned, and the others snickered.

Tobias turned around. "Do you accept Edward and Pete into your pack and promise to protect and care for both of your new pack brothers?"

"Yes" went up in near unison.

"Then I welcome both of you to our pack and family." Tobias leaned forward and lightly scraped Pete's cheek with a claw, drawing a small amount of blood. He didn't do that to Edward, but he did kiss him on the forehead. "We are all brothers and sisters, and we exist and thrive because we work together. We have a good life in what can be a harsh land. So we also thank the Mother for all her gifts, as well as her protection."

"Can we eat now?" Brick asked, and everyone laughed and made for the large table that Clarie had set up and that was groaning under the weight of her cooking.

Pete sat down with Edward, and Lorraine brought him a plate and sat next to him.

"You don't need to hold him if you don't want to."

"He's no problem." Pete turned his head as Tobias sat on his other side, and Pete leaned against him as everyone ate. He ate slowly so as not to disturb Edward.

After the late dinner, the fire was lit, and it blazed to the sky. Everyone sat talking and laughing well into the night. Sasha and Lorraine were the first to leave, with a sleeping Edward, going inside to get some much-needed rest. Clarie, Hayden, and Elayne followed, and Greg and Brick took off to run. Then it was just three of them.

"Go on, you two. I'll make sure the fire is out before I turn in." Ryan shooed them away, and Pete took Tobias's hand and let Tobias lead him inside to their room.

Pete was happy. He had a family and he belonged. That was all he wanted.

Tobias closed the bedroom door, and they climbed into bed and made love until they were both exhausted. They fell asleep curled together, arms and legs entwined.

HAD THEY still been awake, they might have seen the soft glimmer of light in the corner of the room.

"I'm sure as heck glad that not all my children are as big a pain in the ass as you two." The Mother smiled. "You both have my blessings. Now be happy." She was already beginning to fade as her words drifted away on the night breeze.

DIRK is very much an outside kind of man. He loves travel and seeing new things. Dirk worked in corporate America for way too long and now spends his days writing, gardening, and taking care of the home he shares with his partner of more than two decades. He has a master's degree and all the other accessories that go with a corporate job. But he is most proud of the stories he tells and the life he's built. Dirk lives in Pennsylvania in a century-old home and is blessed with an amazing circle of friends.

Facebook: www.facebook.com/dirkgreyson
E-mail: dirkgreyson@comcast.net

YELLOWSTONE WOLVES

CHALLENGE the DARKNESS

Dirk Greyson

Yellowstone Wolves: Book One

When alpha shifter Mikael Volokov is called to witness a
challenge, he learns the evil and power-hungry Anton Gregor will
stop at nothing to attain victory. Knowing he will need alliances to
keep his pack together, Mikael requests a congress with the nearby
Evergreen pack and meets Denton Arguson, Evergreen alpha, to ask
for his help. Fate has a strange twist for both of them, though, and
Mikael and Denton soon realize they're destined mates.

Denton resists the pull between them—he has his own pack
and his own responsibilities. But Mikael isn't willing to give up. The
Mother has promised Mikael his mate, told him he must fight for him,
and that only together can they defeat the coming darkness. When
Anton casts his sights on Denton's pack, attacks and sabotage follow,
pulling Denton and Mikael together to defeat a common enemy. But
Anton's threats sow seeds of destruction enough to break any bond,
and the mates' determination to challenge the darkness may be their
only saving grace.

www.dreamspinnerpress.com

YELLOWSTONE WOLVES

DARKNESS
THREATENING

Dirk Greyson

Sequel to *Challenge the Darkness*
Yellowstone Wolves: Book Two

Fredrik is back from college and trying to stay out of his power-hungry brother's way, until his brother takes a prisoner for his pleasure. Unable to tolerate his family's cruelty, Fredrik overcomes his fear to help her escape back to her pack. There, he meets Christopher, and their instant attraction tells him Christopher is the one. However, since the threat of his brother remains, Fredrik is reluctant to pursue a relationship.

Christopher is still figuring out his place in the pack and has been living on his own to avoid making waves with his brother, Mikael. Now he's met his soulmate, and he'll do anything to take care of his love, including rejoining the pack.

With coaxing, Fredrik accepts his feelings, and Christopher's pack gives him the home he's never had. But Fredrick soon realizes he should keep running. His brother is on his tail and will stop at nothing to obtain the power he craves, especially when he realizes the source of the power could be Fredrik himself.

www.dreamspinnerpress.com

DIRK GREYSON
DAY AND KNIGHT

Day and Knight: Book One

As former NSA, Dayton (Day) Ingram has national security chops and now works as a technical analyst for Scorpion. He longs for fieldwork, and scuttling an attack gives him his chance. He's smart, multilingual, and a technological wizard. But his opportunity comes with a hitch—a partner, Knighton (Knight), who is a real mystery. Despite countless hours of research, Day can find nothing on the agent, including his first name!

Former Marine Knight crawled into a bottle after losing his family. After drying out, he's offered one last chance: along with Day, stop a terrorist threat from the Yucatan. To get there without drawing suspicion, Day and Knight board a gay cruise, where the deeply closeted Day and equally closeted Knight must pose as a couple. Tensions run high as Knight communicates very little and Day bristles at Knight's heavy-handed need for control.

But after drinking too much, Day and Knight wake up in bed. *Together*. As they near their destination, they must learn to trust and rely on each other to infiltrate the terrorist camp and neutralize the plot aimed at the US's technological infrastructure, if they hope to have a life after the mission. One that might include each other.

www.dreamspinnerpress.com

FLIGHT OR FIGHT

POLICE LINE DO NOT CROSS   POLICE LINE DO NOT

DIRK GREYSON

Life in the big city wasn't what Mackenzie "Mack" Redford expected, and now he's come home to Hartwick County, South Dakota, to serve as sheriff.

Brantley Calderone is looking for a new life. After leaving New York and buying a ranch, he's settling in and getting used to living at a different pace—until he finds a dead woman on his porch and himself the prime suspect in her murder.

Mack and Brantley quickly realize several things: someone is trying to frame Brantley; he is no longer safe alone on his ranch; and there's a definite attraction developing between them, one that only increases when Mack offers to let Brantley stay in his home. But as their romance escalates, so does the killer. They'll have to stay one step ahead and figure out who wants Brantley dead before it's too late. Only then can they start the life they're both seeking—together.

www.dreamspinnerpress.com

PLAYING
WITH
FIRE

DIRK GREYSON

Jim Crawford was born wealthy, but he turned his back on it to become a police officer. Add that to his being gay, and he's definitely the black sheep of the family.

Dr. Barty Halloran grew up with lessons instead of friends and toys and as a result, became a gifted psychologist… with only an academic understanding of people and emotions.

When Jim's pursuit of a serial killer goes nowhere, he turns to Dr. Halloran for help, and Barty thinks he can get inside the shooter's mind. In many ways, they're two sides of the same coin, which both scares and intrigues him. Together, Jim and Barty make progress on the case—until the stakes shoot higher when the killer turns his attention toward Barty.

To protect Barty, Jim offers to let Barty stay with him, where he discovers the doctor has a heart to go along with his brilliant mind after all. But as they close in on their suspect, the killer becomes desperate, and he'll do anything to elude capture—even threaten those closest to Jim.

www.dreamspinnerpress.com

www.ingramcontent.com/pod-product-compliance
Lightning Source LLC
Chambersburg PA
CBHW060058260626
47160CB00005B/1706

* 9 7 8 1 6 3 5 3 3 4 1 5 9 *